Tracey V Bateman
AUTHOR
Beside Still Waters
TITLE

DATE DUE	BORROWER'S NAME

Heartsong Presents

Dedicated to Tracie Peterson. Thank you for everything.

A note from the Author:
I love to hear from my readers! You may correspond with me by writing:

Tracey V. Bateman
Author Relations
PO Box 721
Uhrichsville, OH 44683

ISBN 1-59310-800-1

BESIDE STILL WATERS

All scripture quotations, unless otherwise noted, are taken from the King James Version of the Bible.

Our mission is to publish and distribute inspirational products offering exceptional value and biblical encouragement to the masses.

PRINTED IN THE U.S.A.

"Eva, wait."

Jonesy stepped forward and held on to Patches's bridle. He towered over her, and Eva had to cock her head to meet his gaze. "I just want you to know. . ."

He swallowed hard, and so did Eva. "You want me to know what?"

He shrugged. "I don't even know what to say. I've never met anyone like you."

Eva's heart pounded in her ears. "I've never met anyone like you either."

The depth of his gaze left little doubt in Eva's mind that he was being sincere. Usually when a man shared his feelings like this, it meant a proposal was forthcoming. But she knew that wasn't going to be the case with Jonesy. Bracing herself, she nodded her encouragement.

Clearing his throat, he looked away and fingered Patches's bridle. "The thing is, Eva, I'm not staying in Oregon. I can't get tangled up with a woman and take a chance you could talk me out of my dream."

Eva gasped at his assumption that she had any desire to talk him out of leaving. "For your information, Mr. Jones, I have no intention of entangling myself with you. So don't flatter yourself."

"Maybe I'm the only one thinking along the lines of what might be between us, then?"

Drawing a long, slow breath, Eva took a chance. "No. You're not the only one. I just don't see the point of bringing it up when you've made your position so crystal clear."

"I enjoy your company. I'd like us to be friends."

"Without any chance of romantic notions, is that right?"

He nodded. "Is that too presumptuous of me?"

"We can be friends." She squared her shoulders and tamped down the disappointment. After all, she barely knew him. But so far, he was the only man whose company she truly enjoyed.

TRACEY V. BATEMAN lives with her husband and four children in southwest Missouri. She believes in a strong church family relationship and sings on the worship team. Serving as vice president of American Christian Romance Writers gives Tracey the opportunity to help new writers work toward their writing goals. She believes she is living proof that all things are possible for anyone who believes, and she happily encourages anyone who will listen to dream big. E-mail Tracey at tvbateman@aol.com, or visit her Web site at www.traceybateman.com.

Books by Tracey V. Bateman

HEARTSONG PRESENTS

HP424—Darling Cassidy
HP468—Tarah's Lessons
HP524—Laney's Kiss
HP536—Emily's Place
HP555—But for Grace
HP588—Torey's Prayer
HP601—Timing Is Everything
HP619—Everlasting Hope
HP631—Second Chance
HP652—A Love So Tender

one

Spring 1880

Eva's chest swelled with exhilaration as Patches raced across the open field, his hooves throwing chunks of earth in his wake. Clinging to her beloved pinto's neck, Eva tossed a delighted laugh into the dewy air. She'd been in such a hurry to greet the day that she hadn't bothered to saddle or bridle her faithful friend. But she knew he didn't mind. Patches looked forward to their morning runs as much as she did.

The eastern sky exploded with orange, pink, and blue. Eva wished it were possible to ride straight into the horizon and lose herself in such beauty. A pity the earth was round. How wonderful might it be to ride clear to the edge of the world and stop just short of falling off?

At eighteen years of age, Eva knew everyone expected her to stop her wild ways, find a nice young man, settle down, and raise a gaggle of babies. Hadn't she received that sentiment from just about every dowager in town? The consensus of the Ladies' Auxiliary of Hobbs, Oregon, seemed to be that time was passing her by.

Eva wanted to settle down. Eventually. But so far, every time she thought she might be in love, her hopes had been dashed by some foolish act on the part of the young man who had looked so promising. She'd come close to the altar three times—and each time backed out just before making a dreadful, permanent mistake.

Even Ma agreed with the townsfolk. If Eva didn't accept one of her many proposals and actually go through with a marriage soon, she might as well take a teaching position somewhere and resign herself to spinsterhood. She shuddered at the thought. Not the spinster part, the teacher part. She'd tried teaching. Had lasted one week. How on earth could a person stay locked up inside all day, every day, when there was such a marvelous world outside just waiting to be admired and enjoyed?

Ma didn't understand, Eva's sisters didn't understand, none of the females she knew understood, except possibly Cousin Aimee, who had waited until she was twenty-seven years old before she married. Her wedding had taken place two years ago, and she was happier than any bride Eva had ever seen. So Eva saw no reason to rush. And with Pa on her side, she had at least two allies.

By the time horse and rider reached the river, Eva's heart was nearly bursting from her chest and Patches was slobbering like a rabid dog. The pony didn't bother to stop at the water's edge. Instead he walked right into the shallow water and dipped his neck.

Eva laughed and gave him a pat. Her hand came away slick with his sweat. "I'm a bit parched myself, old boy. I suppose I could do with a handful of the river." She swung her leg around, preparing to slide from the horse's back, just as a massive, hairy dog darted into the water, nipping at Patches's legs. The horse reared up, sending Eva splashing into the river.

Patches landed and began running along the embankment. Eva sputtered in the two-foot-deep water, sitting back on her hands, her knees up, feet planted on the riverbed. "Wha—"

The tail-wagging beast chased Patches a few yards upriver, then halted as a shrill whistle split the air.

"Lord Byron," a man's voice commanded. "Get yourself back here."

Eva glanced up. Her heart picked up speed as long, muscled legs waded through the water. Eva looked up as the handsome stranger bent and extended a hand. Eva scooted away from him. How many times had Pa warned her not to be friendly with strange men? The dog reached them just then and gave her a wet lick up the entire length of her cheek.

"Disgusting." Eva wiped her face with the back of her hand and pushed at the dog with the other. His massive paw caught the gold locket around her neck and yanked it off. It landed in the water, and the river swept it downstream.

"No!" Dread paralyzed her, and she remained where she sat. With a groan, she stared after her most precious possession.

"Hold on, I'll get it." The stranger splashed through the water. "There it is." He dove in and came up holding out a closed fist. "Got it!"

Relief flooded her as she took the locket and held it close. "Thank you, sir. This was a gift from my pa the day I was baptized. I've had it since I was twelve."

He wrung out his shirt and swiped dark locks of hair back from his forehead. "My pleasure. And the least I could do since my dog is the one who caused the locket to come loose in the first place. Not to mention your current position in the river *and* scaring your horse away."

As if trying to make amends, the dog gave her another lick. "Oh, for pity's sake."

"Get back, Lord Byron," the stranger commanded. "I'm sorry about that crazy dog. Here, let me help you up."

"No thanks, I can do it myself. You just keep that beast of yours from knocking me down again."

He extended his hand anyway.

"I mean it. I don't accept aid from strange men. And if you come any closer, I'll scream loud enough to make your ears bleed."

His eyebrows rose. "Ah, a spirited young miss," he said in an English accent—obviously put on, since he'd spoken with a perfectly normal accent only seconds before. Something about his tone and the amusement sparkling in his deep blue eyes gave her the unsettling feeling that this man was making fun of her.

As much as she wished to simply toss her head and refuse to speak to him, her curiosity got the better of her. "Where are you from?"

"Texas." His white-toothed smile dazzled in the morning sun.

Eva sniffed. "Then why were you trying to sound like a foreigner?"

"I was teasing. Sorry." He rubbed his palm against his thigh, then reached down again. "Come on, let me help you up," he said in a decidedly Texas drawl. Then he added, in that strange English accent, "I promise I'm not going to try anything, lest your scream cause my ears to run red with blood."

Was this man daft?

Once more she spurned his help. She struggled to her

feet, her face burning as she realized how awkward she must look trying to stand up in the water while maintaining her modesty.

"Suit yourself," he said. He saluted her, and she noticed that he held a book in his other hand. "Just trying to be mannerly, considering my beast is the one responsible for your precarious position."

There he went with that highfalutin talk again. It was enough to make her head spin. Still, as she stood in the shin-deep water, she took a moment to look him over. Broad chest, square jaw, and deep blue eyes that made her legs weak didn't quite match up with a man given to books. Only weak men liked to read, in her experience. This fellow looked like a romantic hero described in the dime-store novels her best friend, Lily, liked to snatch from the shelves of her pa's general store.

He cleared his throat, and she realized she'd been staring. Heat spread across her cheeks.

"I've never seen you around here before," she said, wading past him toward the bank.

He followed. "My family just settled here from Texas last month. Bought a few acres just to the south."

Eva's stomach dropped. What did he mean by "family"? Was he married with half a dozen children? Though she was dying to ask, she couldn't drum up the courage. Instead she simply smiled. "The old Winston place. I'd heard they were selling, but I didn't know anyone had bought it. They never were much to attend town functions or church."

She stepped up onto the bank. A beautiful chestnut mare, tied to a nearby tree, blinked at her. Eva turned and caught the stranger's eye. "I haven't seen you. . .or your, uh, wife at services."

"Haven't left the house much. Still settling in. And I'm not married." He winked, making Eva's cheeks burn. "I suppose Ma'll talk Pa into attending soon. She's getting lonesome for Christian company."

"But not you?"

He captured her gaze, as though he knew she thought him about the most magnificent-looking man she'd ever seen. Interest flickered in his eyes, or perhaps curiosity. But definitely something that went beyond mere politeness.

Eva hurried to clarify. "I mean, for your soul's sake, of course. You don't want to stay out of church very long. Believe me, I know how easy it is to fall into sinful ways."

"I'm sure your sins were many and of the most sordid kind." He made no effort to hide a grin.

Why, he wasn't a gentleman at all! Eva didn't care how handsome he was. It was obvious this man had not been properly raised. "There are sins of the heart and mind just as there are actual hands-on sins. Didn't you know that?"

There. Turn the tables on him. Make him feel as though she thought him a complete idiot.

Only he didn't appear a bit shamed by her chastisement. His eyes crinkled with silent laughter. And then he winked.

Oh my! Eva's eyes widened, and a crushing retort danced on the tip of her tongue, but the stranger spoke up first.

"And pray tell, what were these inward sins that blackened your heart against the goodness of God?" He pressed his hands to his chest in what Eva could only consider to be mockery.

Anger, for instance, and mean thoughts. Not unlike those

tainting her heart at this moment. But she had no intention of revealing such things to this man.

"That is between myself and my Lord," she fumed.

"I can respect that." His eyes sobered. "A person has a right to private thoughts." He looked deep into her eyes, as though sharing a soul-changing moment.

Confusion clouded Eva's mind, along with the sudden, unsettling realization that she didn't really know what he was talking about.

She rarely took much time out for inner reflection beyond her time with God. She was who she was. She served God with the same gusto she did everything else. Her personal Bible times in the old gazebo Uncle Michael had built for Aunt Star deepened her love and faith. And at times, her soul flew away on the wings of praise.

But she hated attending church. The confinement indoors, the drawn-out prayers and lengthy sermons that left her squirming on her seat until Ma's scowling expression told her to be still.

She never could quite understand why people felt they needed to erect a building to put God into anyway. As far as she was concerned, they should hold services outdoors, in the nature God had created, instead of in a stuffy building that was cold in the winter and stifling in the summer.

Still, she felt it her duty as a Christian to inquire as to why this man hadn't included himself when he said his ma and pa would most likely come to church.

"I hope we see you at the service today," she said softly. Which, judging from the placement of the sun in the sky, was set to begin in just a couple of hours.

"Do you?" He smiled. Eva had to admit he could be charming when there was no mockery in his eyes.

Still, his bold assumption that there was anything personal in the statement sent her defenses rising. "Of course I do. I'm concerned for anyone who doesn't attend services on the Lord's Day."

"Are you sure that's all?" His lips twisted, and all the charm left his smile.

Oh, he was baiting her. She recognized a teasing challenge. Didn't she have two older brothers? She knew the best course of action would be to ignore his implication, yet she couldn't help but allow her rising defenses a voice.

Eva sniffed. "If you're trying to imply that I have personal motives, then you're sadly mistaken, Mr. . . ." Eva searched her mind. She didn't even know his name. Only an ill-bred man would allow this much time to pass without so much as offering his name and requesting hers.

Perhaps he didn't care to know her name. The thought grated.

"Jones," he supplied. "Benjamin Jones. But my friends call me Jonesy."

Eva felt his challenge. If she called him Jonesy, he would laugh at her assumption that he wanted to be her friend. "Well, Mr. Jones, there is nothing personal in my query. It was simply a Christian invitation for you to join our fellowship."

"Very well, Miss. . ." His brow rose, and his boyish grin melted Eva's irritation.

She smiled and held out her hand. "Riley. Eva Riley."

Instead of a polite shake, Jonesy lifted her hand and pressed warm lips to her fingers. She caught her breath and jerked back. "As I said, Mr. Jones, my query was not of a personal nature."

"Very well, Miss Riley. Although I must admit my pride is wounded." His eyes continued to sparkle in amusement. "I suppose it's just as well you hold no personal interest," he said boldly. "I'm only staying in Oregon long enough to help Pa get the farm producing. Then I'm going back to Texas to start my own ranch."

Eva ignored the sudden disappointment pinching her insides because he wouldn't be around long enough for her to really get to know him. Honestly, men and their land. What difference did it make? All she needed was a wide-open space to run Patches.

Patches! At the thought of her companion, she looked about, searching for any sign that he'd come back. That wretch of a horse had run off and left her at the mercy of a strange man and his overgrown beast. Home was a good five miles away. And she didn't relish the walk. Ma would skin her alive for being late to breakfast. Especially on the Lord's Day.

Patches would certainly not be receiving a sugar treat today. The coward.

"I suppose I should be going home," she announced. "I'm sure my horse will arrive there soon and everyone will worry." She pushed damp curls from her cheeks and nodded to the handsome stranger.

She could only imagine what she must look like. She hadn't even taken time to braid her hair this morning but had merely tied it back with a ribbon—which now floated down the river. "Good day, Mr. Jones. It was. . .interesting meeting you."

Jonesy. She liked how it sounded in her mind. The name suited his rugged looks. Scratchy stubble lined his jaw. Some men might have appeared unkempt without a full beard or a clean-shaven face, but not this one. His deep blue eyes and thick dark hair caused Eva to swallow hard. Wait until she told Lily.

"It was lovely meeting you, Miss Riley. I'm sorry about my dog. I'm afraid Lord Byron is rather short on manners."

"Why do you call your dog Lord Byron?"

A chuckle rumbled in his chest as he dropped to the ground and removed his boots. "Simple. He likes to sit and listen to me read the poetry of Lord Byron." He turned his boot upside down. Water poured out.

Poetry? Eva couldn't abide poetry. Mooning men and women extolling their true loves. It made her positively ill. She'd rather read a dime-store novel. At least those were entertaining.

Eva's soaked skirt was cooling off with the early morning breeze, and she shivered. "Well, good day."

"How far are you from home?"

She waved her hand in front of her. "Only about five miles. I can walk it in no time."

"It would be my honor to escort you home on Lady Anne." He cocked his head. "I named her after Lord Byron's wife."

Eva smirked. "Does she also enjoy poetry?"

"Naturally. She thinks I'm reading about her beauty." He pressed his index finger lightly to his lips. "Don't speak too loud; she might overhear. I don't want to insult her. She's quite vain."

"You have my word; she will never hear from my lips that

she isn't the subject of the poems."

Jonesy pressed his hand to his heart and gave an exaggerated bow. "Thank you, kind lady. I am forever in your debt. Therefore, you must allow me to give you a ride home on the back of my horse."

The thought of riding so close to him sent a wave of heat to her stomach. Ma wouldn't approve.

She shook her head. "No. I can't accept, though it was kind of you to offer."

"I understand. It might not be proper." He frowned in thought. "Then you must take my horse."

A gasp escaped her throat. "Why, I can't do that. How will you get home?"

"The same way you planned to. The two strong legs God bestowed upon me."

"So you do believe in God."

"Never said I didn't."

He made her positively dizzy. "Regardless, I can't take your horse."

"I live less than a mile from here. It only makes sense."

Eva narrowed her gaze. "Not to me, it doesn't. It's your horse. Mine ran off. You've no obligation to see me home. I can take care of myself."

"I'm walking home. If you don't take Lady Anne, she will feel abandoned and may never recover from the tragedy."

"Why should that matter to me? She's your horse." Eva shrugged and turned to go, but her conscience got the better of her. "I wouldn't leave her alone if I were you. There's been some horse thieving going on in these parts lately. Your lovely mare probably wouldn't be here when you got back."

His brow went up, and Eva noted a flicker of uncertainty in his eyes. It left as quickly as it had come. He shrugged. "I suppose that's a chance I'll have to take."

He was bluffing. Eva knew he must be. "Suit yourself." Her shoulders squared, she turned and began walking toward home, sufficiently confident that she'd won the battle.

"Farewell, my sweet lady. . . ." Jonesy's voice, in that fake English accent, caused her to falter a step. She turned back and scowled. He wasn't speaking to her but to the horse.

"You've been a grand companion," he said, stroking her mane, "and I shall miss you terribly. But I would never be able to live with myself knowing I'd sent a young woman off to trudge her way home across the harsh land while I rode comfortably on your strong back."

Eva rolled her eyes. He must be joking. Surely he wouldn't leave Lady Anne behind after she'd told him about the horse thieves.

Then again, this man seemed daft enough to do it, just to prove a point. "All right, you win."

He looked at her and grinned, not even trying to be gracious in victory. "Excellent. I'll meet you and your family at service this morning and retrieve my beautiful mare."

Eva suddenly realized that accepting his offer would give her a chance to see him again. Smiling to herself, she accepted the reins from his strong, calloused hands.

Eva tried not to read too much into the brush of his fingers against hers. Her mind whirled with the events of the past few minutes as she mounted Lady Anne and nudged the mare into a trot.

Finally she'd met a man who might hold her interest, and

he had no plans to stay in Oregon! Eva took a deep breath and made a firm decision. She would return Lady Anne to him and never again think about his deep blue eyes or full lips. As far as she was concerned, all thoughts of Jonesy as a suitable companion or possible mate were strictly forbidden.

two

Jonesy faced in the direction of his house, opened his book of poetry, and tried to lose himself in the words as he walked home. In an uncommon lack of focus, he stared at the print on the page, but the capacity to form sentences from the disjointed words seemed to escape him. Instead his mind conjured up the image of Miss Riley.

"Eva." The name tasted sweet on his lips, and he felt an unsettling stirring in his breast. Tucking the book under his arm, he replayed every word of their conversation. Her bedraggled appearance after taking that toss in the river had been plenty enchanting in an outdoorsy sort of way.

He chuckled to himself, remembering her dire warning about the temptations of sin. Though he highly doubted she had anything to worry about, she did have a point. Even with daily Bible reading and prayer with his family after supper each night, he was more than ready for a service with fellow believers.

By the time he reached home, the sun had burned the dew from the grass and the delicious smells of bacon and freshly baked biscuits wafted from the house. The door was open to allow in the morning breeze. Jonesy stepped across the threshold.

The sight of his parents locked in an embrace in front of the stove brought a rush of heat to his cheeks. His mother gently pushed out of her husband's arms when she noticed

Jonesy standing in the room. She reached up and patted her hair, giving her son an embarrassed smile.

"I was beginning to wonder if you'd been swept away to some magical kingdom again by one of those books of yours." Her tone rang with amused scolding. "Good thing your pa stood up for you. I was just about to feed your breakfast to Sally Mae and her piglets."

Jonesy tossed a quick glance at his father. Elijah Obadiah Jones stood six feet two, a full head taller than Jonesy's mother, and the difference was never quite as noticeable as when she stood in the crook of his arm, looking up at him with adoration.

Her slender, work-hardened fingers rested on Elijah's chest, and her eyes squinted with fondness. "Of course, your pa's an old softy. He insisted we give you a few more minutes."

Jonesy smiled. "Thanks, Pa."

Elijah tightened his grip on his wife's shoulders and drew her closer. "I wasn't about to let her feed my son's breakfast to an old sow."

Contentment swelled Jonesy's chest. His parents shared a deep love. Either would have moved heaven and earth to make the other happy. He knew love was the only reason Ma had agreed to leave a prosperous ranch and move the three younger children all the way to Oregon so Pa could fulfill his sudden desire to give up ranching and try his hand at farming.

Jonesy stopped by the washbasin and splashed water on his face. "Sorry I'm late, Ma."

"I declare, son." She eyed him up and down and shook her head, giving an exasperated huff. "What happened to you?"

"Lord Byron scared a young lady's horse, and she ended up in the river. I waded in and tried to help her."

"Tried?" Pulling away from her husband's arm, she grabbed a plate and began dishing up breakfast. "What's that supposed to mean?"

He felt a dumb grin spread across his face. "She's feisty. Threatened to scream loud enough to make my ears bleed if I so much as laid a finger on her."

"How ungrateful!" His mother's brow furrowed with indignation, but a chuckle left his pa's throat.

Moving behind his wife, Pa kissed her cheek. "Sounds like your ma in her younger days. She was a feisty little thing herself. Watch out for this one, son. She might just snag you into marriage. Like your ma here did me."

Ma turned with plate in hand and rolled her eyes as she moved past him toward the table. A harrumph escaped her throat. "Your pa chased me until I finally let him escort me to the Christmas dance, just to make him stop asking."

"Yep, and that's all it took. We were married three months later."

Ma set the plate on the table. "Come eat your breakfast, son, so we're not late to services."

"Yes, ma'am." Jonesy sat down and took a whiff of the bacon, eggs, and biscuits with great appreciation. "And you don't need to worry about any woman snagging me. I'll be back in Texas long before the Christmas dance."

His comment brought an end to the lighthearted atmosphere. Ma gathered a deep breath. Pa cleared his throat. "Well, I suppose I'd best go put on my Sunday meetin' clothes."

Regret seared Jonesy as he watched his father leave the room. "Sorry, Ma."

"Oh, son, there's no need to apologize. We're just thankful you came to help out for as long as we can keep you here." She patted his shoulder. "I suppose I'll get myself ready, too. Rinse your plate when you finish, please."

Jonesy nodded. He hated to disappoint his parents. But he had to live his own life. And with his brothers Terrance and Frank, both almost grown, Pa would have plenty of help with the farm. Besides, what did Jonesy know about farming? He'd been raised on a ranch. Just because Pa had decided he'd had enough of ranching and wanted to try his hand at farming, that didn't mean Jonesy had to do the same.

An hour and a half later, the family approached the little white church building in the town of Hobbs. Jonesy had visited town several times to pick up supplies from the general store, and he'd eaten a few meals at Joe's Restaurant. Not bad. But certainly couldn't hold a candle to Ma's cooking.

He rode next to his ma on the seat while Terrance and Frank rode on horseback. Twelve-year-old Dawn sat demurely in the back of the wagon, being the perfect little girl she'd always been. A real young lady. Nothing like the spirited woman he'd met this morning.

Jonesy's heart picked up a beat at the memory of those soft brown eyes rimmed with bristly dark lashes. Her skin had a bronze hue. Most of the young women he knew tried desperately to keep their skin shaded from the darkening effects of the sun. Quite a feat in Texas. But this woman didn't even seem aware of those sorts of things. Or if she was, she didn't bother herself with matters such as darkened or freckled skin, or wild hair that curled when it got wet.

He scanned the churchyard, which was full of wagons and horses. It seemed the church would be quite full this morning.

A low whistle from Terrance arrested his attention. "Now I understand why you'd loan out the Lady."

"Woo-wee," Frank expounded.

"Boys," Ma admonished.

Jonesy's stomach did a flip-flop at the sight of Eva Riley standing next to Lady Anne. She smiled as she held the mare's reins and waved.

"Eyes full of life and fire," Elijah mused.

Jonesy dragged his gaze from Eva and stared at his pa. "What'd you say?"

"Snappy eyes. Just like your ma." The amusement in his voice, followed by his brothers' laughter, brought heat to Jonesy's cheeks.

"You all hush up and stop teasing Ben." Jonesy's ma had never taken to calling him by the nickname he'd been given by his two older brothers, who had families of their own now and had remained in Texas. The name had stuck with his pa and everyone else. But Ma wasn't to be swayed from the name she and Elijah had bestowed upon their son.

He didn't have a chance to respond to his family's teasing. Eva had drawn close with Lady Anne.

Elijah reined in the team, and the wagon rolled to a halt. Terrance dismounted, his grin telltale. Jonesy stepped between him and Eva before the young man could embarrass her with his teasing brand of humor.

"So I see you are honorable." He swept his Stetson from

his head and smiled, keeping his voice even.

"Honorable?"

"You brought the Lady back to me safe and sound like you said you would."

"Oh." She handed over the reins, her smile tentative. "Yes. Thank you." Her subdued manner took him aback. Was this the same girl who had snapped at him and verbally sparred with him earlier? He allowed his gaze to sweep over her. Chestnut hair, which earlier had been loose and clinging to her face, now swept upward, every strand demurely in place. She wore a modest gown of light blue and moved with grace. "I. . .um. . .appreciate your kindness."

A loud, obvious throat clearing came from next to the wagon, where his parents stood waiting to be introduced. "Oh, Miss Riley, I'd like you to meet my parents, Elijah and Caroline Jones."

Eva smiled with warmth and extended her hand first to his mother, then to his father. "It's a pleasure to meet you both. I'm so glad you've made it to our little fellowship."

His mother, who had been cautiously inspecting Eva, relaxed immediately, and a smile spread across her plump cheeks. "I've been longing for Christian fellowship."

Eva tucked her hand through the older woman's arm. "Come, let me introduce you to my ma. But I warn you, she'll recruit you to make clothing for the children in my uncle's orphanage."

"Oh, how wonderful. I'd be delighted."

Eva whisked his mother away as though she'd known her forever. Jonesy stood back and watched, slack-jawed.

"Those two look about as thick as a couple of newborn

pups." Pa clapped him on the shoulder before following the women.

Ma looked over her shoulder. "Coming, son?" By the look in her eye, Jonesy knew she thought she'd found her ticket to keeping him firmly planted in Oregon.

❧

Eva's mother, Hope Riley, wasn't one to pass up an opportunity to invite a new family in the area to Sunday dinner. So an hour and a half after her brother Gregory finally dismissed the service, Eva found herself sitting across from the most intriguing yet strangest man she'd met in her whole life.

She glanced up and caught Jonesy's gaze. He grinned, and her throat constricted as she tried to swallow a bite of venison roast.

The bite lodged, cutting off her air. Still eye to eye with Jonesy, she pointed at her throat. He frowned, then his eyes widened. He pushed his chair back from the table and shot to his feet as Eva fought for air.

"Son, what on earth are you doing?"

Eva's head began to spin. He pounded her on the back, and she started to cough. Finally she felt the bite begin to move, and her airway cleared.

"Here, drink this," Jonesy said softly. He handed her a glass of water.

She took it gratefully and let the cool liquid soothe her burning throat. "Thank you," she croaked.

"Are you okay?" Hope asked.

Eva nodded. "Fine."

"Thanks to quick thinking from Jonesy here," Eva's pa said, approval ringing in his voice.

Now that she knew she wasn't going to die, Eva couldn't help the embarrassed warmth that spread across her cheeks. "May I be excused, Ma?" she asked, unable to look anyone in the eye. "I'm not very hungry anymore."

"Of course."

Eva rose and came face-to-face with Jonesy, who stood close enough to take her in his arms if he chose to do so. Which, of course, he didn't. And why would she even think such a thing? "Thank you, Mr. Jones. Excuse me, please."

She maneuvered around him and fled outside. Once on the steps, that familiar sense of longing, for what she didn't know, reached into her heart and squeezed until she found herself heading instinctively to the barn. She needed to burn off some energy. And the only way to do that was to saddle up Patches and ride across the open fields. Ma would disapprove of her leaving when they had company. But Pa would understand and would come to her defense.

The pungent odor of hay and horse manure filled her nose as she stepped inside the barn. "All right, Patches, old boy. You don't deserve this ride after the way you left me to the mercy of a perfect stranger this morning, but I need it, so there's no choice." In no time, she saddled the horse and led him through the barn doors.

She stopped short when she came face-to-face with Jonesy.

"Going somewhere?" he asked, raking his gaze over Patches and then back to Eva.

"For a ride."

"Mind if I come along?"

Eva shrugged. "Suit yourself."

"You never know when you might need rescuing."

His teasing tone raised her ire. "I never need to be rescued. I can take care of myself."

Brow lifted, he grinned. "Really? And yet I've been forced to come to your aid not once but twice today."

"Wh–what?" Eva sputtered. She couldn't even try to deny he'd saved her from choking. But twice? "I was having a perfectly nice ride with Patches this morning before your rude dog scared my horse half out of his wits. So if I needed 'rescuing,' as you put it, that was only because your dog can't mind his manners." *Much like his master.*

"I see you've been thinking about it quite a lot. Dare I hope you've been remembering me with affection?" His self-assured grin might have irritated her beyond words, and normally she would have put him in his place with a few well-spoken words and a glare of disdain. However, her traitorous sense of humor bubbled up, and laughter sprang from her like a gusher. "Tell me, Mr. Jones, are you always so sure of yourself?"

"Almost always. Aren't you?"

Eva mounted Patches, trying to decide how to answer. He squinted against the late-afternoon sun as he stared up at her. Eva returned his gaze evenly. "There are two kinds of people, Mr. Jones. Those who know who they are and act accordingly. And those who *act* as though they know who they are."

"And which are you, Miss Riley?"

Eva gave a short laugh. "You have to ask?" She left him to draw his own conclusion and nudged Patches forward.

It took all of her inner strength not to turn around to see if Jonesy was following. Patches strained at the bit, wanting to open up into a full gallop, but Eva kept the reins tight.

What if Lady Anne were too much of a lady to catch up to the pony?

In moments, the sound of a horse's hooves confirmed that Jonesy had indeed saddled the Lady and had every intention of catching up. Eva's competitive nature rose to the surface, and she gave Patches what he'd been craving. She loosened her grip on the reins, and both horses raced across the field toward the river.

Two horses, two riders. Eva laughed out loud from the pure joy of warm wind in her face and the feel of Patches's training muscles against her legs. Her hair fell from its modest trappings and whipped out behind her like a flag blowing in the breeze.

Her laughter stopped, however, when Lady Anne drew close, then came alongside, and finally pulled ahead. The sound of Jonesy's laughter echoed across the field.

Anger burned in Eva, and she urged Patches harder. "Come on, boy. Are you going to let a girl beat you?"

Apparently sensing the challenge, Patches increased his speed. But by the time Patches and Eva reached the river, Lady Anne had already halted and was taking a long drink.

Humiliated, Eva glared at Jonesy's smug face. "We weren't ready."

Laughter exploded from him. "Then I apologize for taking unfair advantage of you and your paint pony."

Was he insulting Patches? Her beloved pinto had been a gift from Pa's trapper friend and his Indian wife. "My horse could win against that mongrel of yours anytime."

"That 'mongrel' comes from a thoroughbred mother and a very respectable wild stallion. The two met after Lady

Anne's mother snuck out of her stall one night and ran to meet up with a wild herd."

Though still smarting from the defeat, Eva couldn't help but see the quality in the lovely brown mare. "She's beautiful." She sent him a half grin. "Sorry for the slight to Her Majesty."

"Don't worry about it. She's not really as arrogant as I made her out to be this morning."

"Unlike you, huh?"

"Me?" He pressed his Stetson over his heart. "I'm truly hurt by that remark."

Behind the words, Eva could see the amusement she'd come to expect from him. Was the man ever serious about anything?

Dismounting, she turned loose of Patches's reins and let him drift into the water for his own drink.

Jonesy led Lady Anne to a nearby bush and wrapped the reins around a branch. He eyed Patches, who had drifted a few yards downstream. "Do you think you'd better go get him?"

Eva followed his gaze. "He'll be fine. He's just wading."

"You're going to let your horse roam after the way he ran off this morning?"

"Lord Byron scared him half to death, or he never would have left me like that."

"Are you ever going to forgive my poor beast?"

"Maybe. . .if you teach him some manners."

"Then I'm afraid he's doomed to be forever in your ill favor."

"There's no hope for him?" Why was it that she tended to fall into playacting so easily with this man?

Jonesy gave a heavy, dramatic sigh. "He's a lost cause. I've resigned myself to a life of apologizing for him."

Eva threw back her head and exploded into throaty laugher. "You're funny, Jonesy Jones."

A flush of pleasure crawled across his face, and he smiled. "I'm sure I'll have all my animals in stitches when I start my own herd."

Instantly sobering at the thought, Eva nodded and turned away. "Patches, come here, boy." She gave a shrill whistle, and the horse trotted back. She took his reins. "We'd best be getting back, Mr. Jones."

"Eva, wait." Jonesy stepped forward and held on to Patches's bridle. He towered over her, and Eva had to cock her head to meet his gaze. "I just want you to know. . ."

He swallowed hard, and so did Eva. "You want me to know what?"

He shrugged. "I don't even know what to say. I've never met anyone like you."

Eva's heart pounded in her ears. "I've never met anyone like you either."

The depth of his gaze left little doubt in Eva's mind that he was being sincere. Usually when a man shared his feelings like this, it meant a proposal was forthcoming. But she knew that wasn't going to be the case with Jonesy. Bracing herself, she nodded her encouragement.

Clearing his throat, he looked away and fingered Patches's bridle. "The thing is, Eva, I'm not staying in Oregon. I can't get tangled up with a woman and take a chance you could talk me out of my dream."

Eva gasped at his assumption that she had any desire to talk him out of leaving. "For your information, Mr. Jones,

I have no intention of entangling myself with you. So don't flatter yourself."

"Maybe I'm the only one thinking along the lines of what might be between us, then?"

Drawing a long, slow breath, Eva took a chance. "No. You're not the only one. I just don't see the point of bringing it up when you've made your position so crystal clear."

"I enjoy your company. I'd like us to be friends."

"Without any chance of romantic notions, is that right?"

He nodded. "Is that too presumptuous of me?"

"We can be friends." She squared her shoulders and tamped down the disappointment. After all, she barely knew him. But so far, he was the only man whose company she truly enjoyed.

Perhaps friendship was all she was cut out for. Maybe she would be an old spinster after all. Just as the town gossips predicted. There were worse things in life. Better to enjoy a friendship with a man who made you laugh than to spend your life married to a man who made you cry.

"Friends, then." He grinned and pressed her shoulder with his palm. He went to retrieve Lady Anne while Eva mounted Patches.

"We'll race you back." She grinned down at him, then nudged Patches into a full gallop.

"Hey, that's cheating," Jonesy called after her.

Eva laughed into the air and gave the horse his head. This time she was determined not to lose.

three

The summer flew by in a variety of fun-filled days, and Eva soon wondered how she ever endured life without Jonesy's friendship. Now that the summer heat had cooled to a lukewarm autumn, she tried to push from her mind the fact that Jonesy would soon be leaving.

Harvest was a busy time, and she'd barely seen him in the past couple of weeks. Desperate for some companionship, Eva jumped at the chance to ride to town for a bag of flour for Pa's birthday cake. At least she could spend a few minutes catching up on town gossip with her best friend, Lily.

She let Patches have his head, and they raced down the road, throwing up dirt and pebbles from the path.

All at once, Patches stumbled. The ground rose up to meet Eva with alarming speed. She landed hard and lay on the road for a moment, trying to get her bearings. Pain jabbed her left hip. She groaned. The blue sky above her came back into focus, and she sat up slowly. In six years, Patches had never once thrown her.

The horse stood at the side of the road, favoring his right front leg. Ignoring the pain in her hip, Eva struggled to her feet and limped to Patches. She patted his neck and slowly moved around to the leg. After a quick inspection, it was clear why Patches had sent her sailing from his back. He'd thrown a shoe.

"I'm sorry, boy. You must have hit a rock and bruised your

hoof. We'll get you fixed up in no time."

Blowing out a breath, Eva glanced down the road, then back toward the direction in which she'd come, debating whether to walk the rest of the way to town or go back home. The distance would be about the same. But in town she'd be able to get the flour Ma needed for Pa's birthday cake. And she could visit the livery stable and have Patches reshoed. She could rent another horse for the ride home and leave Patches there while he healed up from the bruise.

Her mind made up, she took hold of Patches's reins and led him toward town. The September day brought a mild breeze. As Eva walked along the road, she lifted her face to the wind, enjoying its soothing caress.

Normally autumn was her favorite time of year, but dread had been her constant companion all summer. The closer harvesttime came, the more aware she was that Jonesy's time in Oregon was almost over. She tried not to think about it, tried to just enjoy their time together. Taking long rides along the river's edge, sitting in the gazebo while Jonesy read poetry to her. She was even learning to tolerate some of the wounded-heart cries from scorned loves.

Jonesy had made a valiant attempt to read one of her dime-store novels, but he'd declared it to be the downfall of cultured literature.

Eva smiled at the memory. She'd tried not to show how much she was beginning to love him. Of all the men who had courted her, professed love for her, sought to marry her, Jonesy was the one who had finally caused her to surrender to love. And her heart belonged to a man who loved his dream of owning a ranch in Texas more.

Familiar daydreams began to filter through her mind. . . .

Her wearing a wedding gown. Jonesy reading poetry aloud at the end of a long day of working in the fields. But he had his own dream. And that dream didn't include marrying a girl who would tie him down to a land he didn't love.

What Jonesy apparently didn't realize was that Eva would follow him anywhere. To Texas or the ends of the earth. Besides, there was something exciting in the possibility of scratching a living in a new land. Building from the ground up. Starting with nothing and ending up prosperous, the way her parents had.

Of course, her ma had been wealthy when she'd met Pa, but they still had to work together. Pa was a craftsman, not a farmer. His furniture sold widely, and now they were one of the most prosperous families in the state. He'd done that on his own, Ma's money notwithstanding. And though Eva's older half brother, Greg, and twin half brother and sister, Billy and Betsy, all had large inheritances from their own pa's estate back in Chicago, Eva's inheritance would be just as great. Her pa had seen to that.

Caught up in her thoughts and the enjoyment of being outdoors in the cool fall day, Eva didn't notice the sound of horses' hooves until it was too late to duck into the woods and hide herself. She stopped and waited as three men approached.

Please, Lord, let them go on past.

"Well, look at this, boys. What do we have here?"

Eva's stomach churned at the man's gruff voice. He spat a stream of tobacco juice and narrowly missed the hem of her skirt. Her knees grew weak under the lecherous scrutiny of the three men.

Still, if there was one thing Pa had taught her about

dealing with precarious situations like this, it was to never show fear.

"You fellas lost?" Her voice trembled only slightly. She prayed they hadn't noticed.

The second speaker, a younger, thinner man with a scraggly red beard and a mouthful of black or broken teeth, leaned forward in his saddle. "Well, now, what makes you ask a question like that? Don't we look like we belong in these parts?"

"I've lived here all my life and have never seen you. That's all I meant."

Eva felt the third man's dark gaze raking over her. "If we was lost, would you help us get unlost?"

The innuendo in his tone sent warning bells ringing through Eva's mind. She'd heard whispered rumors of what could happen to a woman caught alone on an abandoned road. Her pride had kept her from thinking anything harmful could happen to her. She'd always figured Patches would get her safely wherever she needed to go. He'd only been outrun by one other horse ever: Lady Anne. But there was nothing either of them could do now to avoid what was possibly to come.

Eva tried to form a plan of escape. With Patches injured, running would be futile. If only she carried a pistol! Pa had given her one, but she hadn't bothered to carry it with her. She prayed her arrogance wouldn't get her killed. Or worse.

"Whatsamatter with your horse, little lady?" the first man asked, nodding to Patches.

Eva shrugged, attempting nonchalance. "He threw a shoe. I think he must have a stone bruise, because he keeps limping."

The hulking man dismounted. Eva caught her breath at his sheer size up close. He loomed over her, taller by more than a foot, she was sure. Her stomach dropped. There was no way she could fight off this man. Not in her own strength.

A silent prayer formed in her mind. *Lord, I'm not ready to die. Please send help.*

His meaty hands slid over Patches. "Yes siree, this is one fine horse. I bet he'd bring a good price."

"My horse is not for sale," Eva said, summoning enough courage to give the man a cold tone.

The man turned steely eyes on her. "He ain't, huh?" He gave Patches a pat on the neck. In a flash, a knife appeared in his hand.

Eva gasped and backed up. If she ran down the road, they'd catch her easily on horseback. In the woods, there'd be no chance of anyone finding her and coming to her rescue.

Oh, Lord, what do I do?

He reached his fat hand to her locket and yanked it from her neck.

"Hey! My pa gave me that."

"That was real nice of him. But you won't need it where you're goin'."

"I—I won't?"

"Now, you be a good little girl and be still, and this won't hurt a bit."

"Wh–what won't hurt?"

He gave a wicked laugh. "Don't worry, honey. I only want the horse."

Somehow, knowing she wasn't about to be violated gave her a sense of dignity. She lifted her chin. If there was to be no escape, she would at least die well. Like the Indians Pa so loved and admired. Closing her eyes, she waited for the end to come.

❧

Jonesy took his ma's list of supplies and his pa's instructions to pick up the new wagon wheel from the blacksmith's shop and flapped the reins at the team of horses. The wagon jerked forward and rattled down the road. Jonesy noted the cool air, and his mind began to wander.

Harvest was approaching rapidly. Before long, all the crops would be in. He'd be ready to head home to Texas soon. His brother Theodore was keeping an eye on the one hundred acres of land Pa had given to him—part as inheritance, part in payment for coming to Oregon and helping get the farm started. His end of the arrangement was almost fulfilled.

Jonesy's stomach churned with excitement as it always did at the thought of his own ranch. He'd saved every dime he'd earned as a cowhand on Pa's farm, working since he was sixteen years old. He now had enough to start with a small herd of his own.

The sound of an approaching rider captured his attention. He glanced over his shoulder and waved as he recognized Nathan Compton, a newly married young man with a small ranch a few miles south. He pulled his horse to a stop. Heavy breathing and a wild look in the man's eyes caused Jonesy to tense with anticipation. "What's wrong?"

"My father's ranch. . ." He gulped in a mouthful of air.

"Take it easy," Jonesy interjected. "Slow down and tell me what happened."

"Thieves." Nathan swiped the back of his hand across

his forehead. "Two of Pa's hands were murdered. One got away."

"Did he say how many there were?"

"Said he counted seven."

Seven men shouldn't be too hard to find, provided they stayed together. "How many of your horses did they make off with?"

"No more than five, near as we can figure."

"Five shouldn't be too hard to track."

"These fellas are wily. They've stolen from at least a half-dozen families over the past year, and no one has been able to catch them."

"Then it's time someone did. You headed to the sheriff's office?"

Nathan nodded. "Times like this, I think the farmers have the right idea."

"Why's that?"

"Nothing to steal. Unless you're a bird."

"I'd rather take my chances on a ranch any day." Jonesy flapped the reins, and the horses moved forward. Nathan's mare kept pace.

"Me, too. But seeing Shem and Booker dead like that sure shook me up a mite."

"No one could blame you."

Nathan frowned as he glanced at the road ahead. He jerked his chin. "What's going on up there?"

Jonesy's heart nearly stopped when he noticed Patches standing at the side of the road. Three men, two on horseback. A third one standing over Eva, brandishing a knife, poised to. . . *Oh, Lord, help me.*

"You packing a rifle?" he asked Nathan.

"Yeah, and a pistol, too."

"When I give the signal, fire into the air. Once. Just to get their attention."

Jonesy pulled his pistol from his holster and urged the wagon forward. "Now, Nate."

Gunfire blasted the air. Eva's would-be attackers swung around.

"Throw down your weapons," Jonesy warned the men. He aimed his pistol at the man on the ground next to Eva. "Step away from the lady and drop that knife before I send a bullet into your skull."

"Take it easy now, mister," the man said, tossing his knife into the dirt near his feet. "We didn't mean the girl no harm."

"You filthy, stinking liar!" Eva's outrage shot through the air. "Don't believe him, Jonesy. He was just about to slice my throat."

The man glared at Eva. "You ain't got no proof of that."

"What I saw was proof enough," Jonesy said. "Eva, kick that knife far from his reach, and then come to the wagon."

She did as he instructed. Relief spread through him when she came close enough for him to confirm that she was unharmed. He hopped down and helped her to the seat. He handed her his pistol. Then he pulled some rope from the back of the wagon. "Cover me." He walked halfway to where the three men were—two still on horseback, the other standing in the road.

He looked first at the scraggly-bearded redhead on the black-and-white paint. "All right, Red, slowly dismount and make your way over here. And don't try anything. Nate wouldn't hesitate to shoot."

"Neither would I," Eva called.

Jonesy's lips twitched.

The burly man dismounted, and Jonesy tied his hands behind his back. Jonesy eyed him carefully. "Slowly walk to the wagon."

With a snarl, the bound man shuffled toward the wagon.

"Nate, once he's in there, tie his feet."

"I'll do it," Eva piped up. "Nate needs to cover you."

"No, Eva. Stay away from him." When Jonesy turned to reiterate his words, the other horseman kicked his horse's flanks and took off at a gallop, nearly knocking the third man to the ground.

"Stop!" Nate fired into the air, but the rider didn't slow. "Want me to go after him, Jonesy?"

"No. I'm going to need your help getting these two to the sheriff." He grabbed the knife off the ground, stuffed it into his waistband, then tied up its owner with the remaining rope.

"You're making a big mistake, fella," the man said, squirming. "You ain't got no proof that I did anythin' wrong."

"I saw you standing over this young lady with a knife in your hand."

"He's a horse thief, too." Eva's voice was filled with anger. "I can testify to that."

"Your word against mine, little girl."

"Who do you think my brother, the sheriff, is going to believe?" Eva shot back.

That silenced him.

"And another thing," Eva said, glaring. "Give me back my locket."

Jonesy turned to the thief. "Where is it?"

"In his shirt pocket."

Jonesy reached inside the pocket and retrieved Eva's prized possession.

"It's worthless junk anyway," the man said, spitting on the ground.

Eva gave a sniff. "Then you're a stupid thief."

Jonesy smiled with satisfaction. Eva was one spunky girl. Once, he'd thought he preferred the kind of soft-spoken, demure woman depicted in his beloved poetry. But that was before he met Eva.

The thought of this man threatening her sent anger shooting through him. He finished tying his hands, a little tighter than necessary, then gave him a shove toward the wagon. "We'll get these two situated in a cell, where they belong. Then we can go after the other one. Unless I miss my guess, the one that got away will most likely lead us straight to the rest of the horse thieves."

"You don't know what you're talking about, mister," the redheaded man said. "The rest of the gang's long gone by now."

"Shut up, you idiot," the apparent leader growled.

"That's real interesting information," Nate said with a nod. "I'm sure the sheriff's going to be grateful. He's been trying to catch you rattlesnakes for some time."

❧

Eva still trembled by the time her brother Billy, known as Sheriff Bill Riley to folks in the area, finished questioning her. Fortunately, he determined there was enough evidence to detain the two thieves until the circuit judge rode through.

Her brother wrapped her in a strong hug, then held her

out at arm's length. "You sure you're okay? Do you need to go talk to Gregory? He could pray with you."

"There's no need to bother Greg. It's all over now." Eva smiled with great affection at her brother. "Besides, I have to pick up a bag of flour over at the general store. Ma's making Pa a cake tomorrow. Be sure to come out for some."

A flush spread across her brother's face. "You, uh, going to see Lily?" Though nearly ten years her senior, Billy had never made time to find a wife. Now he seemed enamored of Eva's closest friend, Lily. The storekeeper's pretty little daughter had been waiting so long for him to notice her that she'd almost despaired of finding a husband.

"Yes. Do you have a message for her?"

Jonesy chuckled.

Billy frowned and cleared his throat. "No. Not at all. Why would I? She's your friend, not mine."

"Fine," Eva retorted. "But I wouldn't wait around too much longer if I were you. She's getting awfully tired of holding out for you." Without giving him a chance to answer, Eva looked up at Jonesy. "You ready?"

After a quick farewell to Billy, they stepped out onto the boardwalk. "I'll drop you off at the general store," Jonesy said, "then take Patches to the livery. Would you mind giving Lily my ma's supply list? I could pick up the order when I come to get you, after I get Patches settled in and go see about a wagon wheel at the smithy."

Eva nodded. "I wouldn't mind at all."

Jonesy stopped when they reached the wagon and placed a hand on her arm before she climbed in. "Are you sure you don't want to go talk to the preacher?"

"I'm sure. It's just all so. . .overwhelming." Unbidden tears filled her eyes. Traitorous tears.

"Honey, come here." Jonesy's tender voice washed over her like a warm summer rain, and she willingly went into his arms, despite the curious onlookers. "I praise God that Nathan and I came along when we did."

He stroked her hair, and she was almost sure she felt him press a kiss to the top of her head. Eva snuggled into the embrace, her cheek resting on his solid chest. She closed her eyes as tears squeezed out and ran down her cheeks. For the first time in as long as she could remember, she was afraid to be alone.

"People are beginning to stare. I guess we should get going." Jonesy pushed her slightly from him and reached into his pocket. "Here, take my handkerchief." He assisted her into the wagon.

Shame filled Eva. She felt more helpless than she'd ever felt in her life.

They rode in silence until they reached the general store. "Are you sure you're going to be all right?"

His eyes held such compassion that Eva almost started crying again. She blinked back the tears and nodded. "I'll be fine. I'll just wait for you inside until you return."

Reaching forward, he trailed his thumb along her jawline. His eyes roved over her face. "I'll hurry. And don't worry, Eva. I'm not going to let anything happen to you. Come on, I'll walk you inside."

Eva took his arm, and they stepped into the general store together. He nodded to Lily, who peered at them with curiosity and large eyes that spoke volumes.

"I'll be back later, okay?" His eyes were filled with such concern that Eva couldn't help but smile.

"Don't worry. I won't be afraid while I'm with Lily."

The bell above the door dinged as he departed.

Eva gathered a deep breath and pivoted on her heel to face her wide-eyed friend. She walked toward the counter. "Lovely day, isn't it?"

Lily gave a huff and, ignoring Eva's attempt at diversionary conversation, got straight to the point. "I vow, you two have the strangest relationship. Is Jonesy courting you, or isn't he?"

Eva smiled.

Her friend sighed with exasperation. "Come on, Eva. I'm your best friend in the world. Can't you tell me what's going on?"

Eva shrugged. "I've told you over and over. Jonesy is my friend, and that's where it ends. He only plans to see his pa through the harvest, then he intends to go back to Texas before the winter weather sets in." She bit her trembling lip. Her emotions were so raw that anything might cause her to burst into tears, and she didn't want to do that.

"And he's never tried to hold your hand or steal a kiss?"

"Nope. Not even once."

Lily's blond ringlets bounced as she shook her head. "After all these months, he hasn't changed his mind? I don't know whether to believe that or not. You two looked awfully chummy driving up together. And why did he lead your horse away tied to the back of his wagon?"

Eva couldn't share her experience on the road with her friend. Even as dear as Lily was, the thought of reliving it with words sent a cold trickle of sweat sliding down her spine.

"Patches threw a shoe while I was on my way to town.

Jonesy saw me walking with my horse. Since he needed to pick up a wagon wheel that was being repaired, he kindly agreed to take Patches to the livery."

"I see. So he'll be back to collect you after he's done his manly errands." She wrinkled her nose in amusement. "Sounds very much like a married thing to do."

"Trust me. It's nothing like that."

The look of suspicion on Lily's face expressed her skepticism. "What's that in your hand? Is it a list for me?"

Heat spread across Eva's cheeks. "Jonesy asked me to gather a few supplies for his ma while I'm here."

A delighted smile split Lily's pretty round face. "Oh, Eva. You really are acting like a married couple."

Eva's jaw went slack. "Don't be ridiculous."

Rolling her eyes, Lily held out her hand. "Fine, have it your way. Give me the list."

"Ma needs a five-pound bag of flour, too."

"That all?"

"Yes. She'll come into town for more supplies in a few days, but she wants to do some extra baking for Pa's birthday tomorrow. A mouse got into the pantry."

Lily shuddered. She grabbed the bag from the shelf behind her and dumped it on the counter. "There you go. Now what about Jonesy's list?"

Avoiding eye contact, Eva handed it over. "Any new books?"

"Oh yes, a new shipment arrived a few days ago."

Eva left Lily to fill the order and walked to the display shelf. She glanced over the new selections. Her eye focused on a book of poetry. She couldn't resist picking it up. It didn't mean anything, she tried to convince herself. Not only had Jonesy saved her life, but he would be leaving soon. A going-away present was perfectly acceptable between friends.

Jonesy returned to the general store just as Lily finished filling the order. Eva waved good-bye to Lily, then headed out of town with Jonesy.

The noon sun shone down with much more warmth than earlier in the day. They chatted about everything, it seemed, except what was weighing the heaviest on Eva's mind.

When they approached the spot in the road where she'd nearly been killed earlier, she started trembling. Jonesy took her arm and pulled her to him. "Come here." He slipped his arm around her shoulder. "You're safe with me, honey."

Eva relaxed as the wagon rolled past the fearsome spot in the road. She felt safe with Jonesy.

But what about in another month, when he was gone? Would she ever feel safe again?

❧

From the woods, he watched for a sign that the girl might be riding back alone. When he'd seen her earlier that day, he'd known she was for him. Beautiful dark eyes and dark hair. Long eyelashes. Skin that begged to be stroked. He shuddered as he waited for her.

He never would have let Randy kill her. He'd been just about to step in when those two men had shown up. Fury burned in him at their interference. But at least they'd supplied him with her name. *Eva.* That's what they'd called her.

The sound of a wagon rattling on the road arrested his attention. His heart nearly clogged his throat at the sight of his Eva. He narrowed his gaze as anger scorched out the love he'd felt mere seconds before. She was no better than his mother. No better than all the other women he'd loved.

He watched her lay her head on the man's shoulder. Her betrayal sent shards through his stomach. She would pay for this disloyalty.

four

On the night of the harvest dance, as he dressed for the party, a wretched bit of truth hit Jonesy hard. He'd worked so much the past couple of weeks that he'd forgotten to invite Eva to the last dance he would be attending in Hobbs, Oregon. He couldn't believe he'd never caught the hints. Now he understood why she'd brought it up last Sunday after the church service.

He groaned as he slicked back his hair. It was curling slightly at the ends. Another reason to kick himself. He needed a haircut. But Ma was already dressed for the dance, so he couldn't very well ask her to cut it for him. He raked his fingers through the thick strands and shrugged. It would have to do.

He snatched his Stetson from the hook on his door and headed down the hallway to the kitchen. Since Eva's run-in with the horse thieves, the sheriff had advised folks to travel in groups as much as possible. Jonesy would ride Lady Anne but stay near the wagon with Pa and Ma, as would Terrance and Frank.

"It's about time you got yourself prettied up." Terrance's teasing laughter met Jonesy as he stepped into the front room.

Ma gave him a scrutinizing frown. "Gracious, son, your hair needs a pair of shears, doesn't it?"

"It can wait."

"No, it can't. Now you sit down and let me trim it up. I won't have it said that my sons aren't respectable."

"I'd hate to make you late for the dance."

"Nonsense. Terrance and Frank can go on ahead."

"Ma," Frank said, "we agreed that you wouldn't go anywhere without all of us escorting you. It's safer that way."

Ma waved away his protest. "It's been two weeks since Mr. Compton's horses were stolen, and no one has seen hide nor hair of the rest of those thieves. They're probably long gone by now. I'll be plenty safe with Ben and your pa." She raised up on her dainty toes and pressed a kiss to Frank's cheek. "You're a good son, but I'll be fine."

Frank and Terrance looked at Jonesy for support. In answer to their silent appeal, he smiled at his mother. "Really, Ma. I think I can go out in public one more time without a haircut."

The door opened, and Pa stepped inside. "What's the holdup? The team's all hitched and ready. Are we going to this thing, or ain't we?"

Apparently not the least bit intimidated by her husband's crotchety attitude, Ma waved him to a chair. "Coffee's still warm. Pour yourself a cup while I cut Ben's hair."

"Isn't it a bit late for that?"

"It'll only take a minute if we can get started," she said pointedly.

Pa blew out a breath. "All right. There's no changin' her mind when she's got it set on somethin'." He poured his cup of coffee and glanced at the two teenaged boys. "You two best go along to the dance before Elizabeth McDougal gives up on the both of you and picks some other fellow to dance with."

Jonesy laughed out loud as the competitive young men bounded for the door. The house shook as they slammed the door behind them. Jonesy pulled a wooden chair away from the family table while Ma brought her shears from the kitchen shelf.

"Look at this," she scolded. "I can't believe you were going to take Eva to a dance looking like this."

"I'm not taking her."

"What do you mean?" A frown creased her brow. "Eva's going with some other young man?"

Heat spread across his face. "I don't know. I forgot about it and never asked her."

She gave a huff of indignation. "Do you mean to tell me after all these months of beauing her around, you forgot to ask her to the biggest dance of the year? It'll serve you right if she did take up with someone else."

Mindless of the sharp shears next to his ear, Jonesy turned to look at his mother. "Beauing her around? Eva and I are only friends. She knows what my plans are."

Pa gave a snort from his seat at the table. He swallowed a sip of coffee and spoke evenly. "What a woman knows in her mind and what her heart tells her are two different things."

"What does that mean?"

"He means Eva Riley is in love with you, son. It's as plain as the nose on her face every time she looks at you." Ma's voice gentled. "And unless I miss my guess, you're in love with her, as well."

"Maybe."

A slow smile crept across her mouth. "You're not going to deny it?"

"Nope." Jonesy gave her a grin. Finally admitting his

love for Eva made him feel freer than he'd felt in a long time. "I knew for sure that day on the road. I'd never felt so protective of anyone as I did Eva."

"So what are you going to do about it?"

"I don't know. I have to get back to my land, but Eva's whole life is here. I don't know if I can ask her to leave."

"Maybe you should let her make that decision." She scrubbed his neck with the towel and brushed at his back. "All done. Let's go."

Jonesy kept his thoughts to himself as he rode alongside the wagon on Lady Anne. Some things were just too private to share. Things like whether he could ask Eva to go to Texas with him. In addition to big considerations like leaving her family, it would also mean a quick wedding. That thought sat well with him, but he couldn't be sure how Eva would respond. After all, neither of them had spoken of any feelings beyond friendship. And though he suspected Eva returned his affection, a proposal would still come as a surprise.

Wagons and horses littered the street between Joe Grafton's restaurant at one end of town and the livery stable at the other. The empty lot next to the livery had been transformed into a dance floor, as there was nowhere large enough to hold everyone who would be attending from the town of Hobbs and the surrounding area.

Long poles had been erected at the four corners of the floor and rope strung between them. Hanging lanterns lit up the entire area, including the tables and benches set along the sides of the dance floor. Caleb Owens and Victor Mansfield made up the band: Caleb on the banjo, Victor playing the accordion.

Jonesy tied up Lady Anne to the nearest hitching post and walked the rest of the way to the dance. He scanned the area for any sign of Eva.

He saw the sheriff leaning against a post, sipping punch and watching the dancers. Jonesy came up beside him. "Evenin', Sheriff."

Billy acknowledged him with a nod. "You made it."

"Any reason to think I wouldn't?"

A side grin split his lips. "According to my little sister, you'd better not show up if you know what's good for you." He clapped Jonesy on the shoulder. "You have about as much to learn about women as I do. Only don't wait so long as I did, or you might just end up all alone."

"Yeah, thanks. I'll remember that." He continued his perusal, but the dance floor was so crowded, it was hard to see faces unless they were right in front of him. "Where's Eva?"

"I saw her dancing with Pa a minute or two ago."

"Help me look, will you?" He saw her just as she saw him. Her eyes widened, then narrowed. Her lips pressed together, and she lifted her chin, turning away from him.

So she was going to be stubborn. He'd show her right good and well. He grabbed Billy's arm and strode across the dance floor. The sheriff yanked his arm away. "If you think I'm dancing with you, you're crazy."

"I need you to dance with Eva so I can talk to your pa."

"Pa? Oh, boy. I hope you know what you're doing, because this is going to make Eva right hot under the collar."

"For a little while maybe. But we both know she can't stay mad longer than it takes to saddle a horse."

He chuckled. "From the look on her face, I'm thinking this might be the first time she holds a grudge."

"Don't let him cut in, Pa." Eva's low tone reached Jonesy's ears as her gaze cut through him like a hunting knife.

Andy Riley filled out his buckskin jacket as though he were still a young man, and Jonesy wouldn't have wanted to tangle with him for any reason.

Ignoring Eva's outburst, Jonesy glanced at her pa. "Sir, may I have a word with you?"

Eva sputtered. "You came out here to get my pa to leave me on the dance floor? Why, you. . .you. . .baboon."

Billy took her by the arm. "Take it easy, sis. He brought me along to take Pa's place."

"I don't need you to find me a dance partner, Benjamin Jones. I can find one on my own." Jerking away from Billy, she stomped up to the nearest man, Lily's pa, the owner of the general store. "Dance with me, Mr. Brewster?" She turned to Lily. "You don't mind dancing with Billy, do you?"

Lily flushed, then gave a shy wink of her dimples. "I—if the sheriff doesn't mind, I don't suppose I do."

Billy turned red. "It'd be my pleasure, Miss Lily."

Eva turned to Mr. Brewster. "Well then. Now that that's settled, how about you and me?"

The old-timer scowled. "That was sort of embarrassing for my daughter, Miss Eva."

"Embarrassing?" She took the first step and placed her hand on his shoulder, then waited expectantly for him to do his part. "Mr. Brewster, Lily is my dearest friend. Don't you know I have her best interests at heart? Besides, if you'll dance with me, I'll tell you a secret."

He placed his hand on her waist and took her upraised hand. "What sort of secret?"

Jonesy watched as she charmed the old buzzard.

"My brother Billy has been moon-eyed over your daughter for as long as I can remember. And why do you think she won't look at another young man? She's mooning over him, too. So I did them both a favor."

A smile spread across the wrinkled face. "I see. Then the least I can do is give you this dance." He swung her around and swept her away.

Jonesy and Mr. Riley stood in the middle of the dance floor while dancers whirled past. Some frowned at the two men, others grinned in amusement, all looked curious.

Andy Riley eyed him evenly. "I hope you have a good reason for making a spectacle of my daughter, not to mention the rest of us."

"I tried to make less of a spectacle by bringing Billy along to take over for you."

It would have gone smoothly, too, if Eva weren't so mule-headed. But there was no sense in antagonizing Mr. Riley by being critical of his daughter. Especially now. Even if it was a fact, not to mention common knowledge for anyone who knew her.

"I guess you have a point there," Mr. Riley acknowledged. "Let's get out of everyone's way before they tar and feather us."

When the two men had made it safely through the maze of dancers and found a quiet spot next to a wagon, Mr. Riley faced Jonesy. "Now what do you want that couldn't wait until I was finished dancing with my daughter? Dancing with her for the fourth time, I might add, because it appears all the eligible young men who might have asked her to dance believe you are courting her, and they don't want to move in on another man's girl." Andy folded his arms across his barrel chest. "Suppose you start by telling me why you allowed my daughter to come to a dance alone for the first time since she was thirteen."

Jonesy rubbed his jaw and cleared his throat. "That was purely an oversight, sir. I would have asked her, but I didn't think about it. I just figured we'd show up with our parents like we do for church and then spend the rest of the dance together." He raked his fingers through his newly shorn hair. "I guess I am a baboon, like Eva said."

Laughter rumbled through Andy's chest. "Well, at least the two of you agree on that point. But that's not why you interrupted our dance."

"No, sir." Jonesy shifted from one foot to the other. This was ridiculous. He had no reason to be nervous. He was a grown man, not a boy. Eva was a grown woman and pretty well past the age when most women married anyway. "I intend to ask for Eva's hand in marriage," he blurted out.

Mr. Riley stared and said. . .absolutely nothing.

Jonesy swallowed hard and went on with nervous energy. "I want you to know that I love her and I'll do right by her, if she agrees to marry me."

"Are you saying you plan to stay on and farm after all? Or will you try to build a ranch around here?"

"Well, neither. . . I. . ."

"I see." Mr. Riley's voice dropped. "You want to take my daughter away."

"If she'll have me, then yes, sir. I already own a hundred acres in Texas and have money saved to start my herd. Even have a cabin and a barn, and a small bunkhouse for the cowhands I'll need to hire. I can't up and leave it for good. Any more than I could leave Eva without at least asking her to come with me as my wife."

The hulking man's shoulders slumped. "I see you have your mind made up. I can't say I blame you. As a matter of fact, it shows right good sense and stability on your part." He drew a short breath and nodded. "If my daughter will have a baboon like you, then you have my blessing."

Joy leaped into Jonesy's heart, and he felt like shouting. He grabbed Mr. Riley's hand and pumped it. "Thank you, sir. Thank you very much."

Mr. Riley chuckled. "No need to thank me. Eva will make up her own mind. But I warn you, she's come close to the altar more than once and hasn't gone through with the 'I do' yet."

Jonesy grinned at Mr. Riley. "She will with me."

"We'll see. Now if you don't mind, I'm going to go ask my wife to dance. She's starting to look like a wallflower, and if I don't do something about that, I won't get a decent meal for a week."

Jonesy watched him walk away. Hope Riley, Eva's ma, turned as though sensing her husband was coming. Her face, illuminated by the lantern light, brightened even further at the sight of him.

What would Eva be like in twenty-five years? Loving him. Growing old with him. She was aggravated with him at the moment, but by the end of the evening, she would be his bride-to-be.

❧

Eva stiffened as Jonesy approached her at the refreshment table. It was his fault she was forced to get her own drink in the first place. She sipped her punch and deliberately turned her back to him.

"Eva," he said, in that scolding tone he used when she

was being "stubborn," as he called it.

"I'm not speaking to you, Mr. Jones."

He gave an exasperated huff. "Yes, you are." Taking her by the arm, he led her away from the table.

"How dare you manhandle me?" Eva demanded, but she didn't pull away from him. It was rather thrilling for him to be acting this way. Like more than just a friend. "I've half a mind to tell my pa and just see what he does to you."

"Tell him. He's dancing with your ma."

"Well, what do you want? I don't want to leave the dance, although no one is dancing with me but my family."

"Listen, Eva." He stopped short and spun her around to face him. "I'm sorry I didn't ask you to the dance. I just didn't think about it."

Eva sniffed. "You and all your romantic poetry. Hasn't it taught you anything?"

Heat crawled across her cheeks. She hid her embarrassment behind what she hoped was a nonchalant shrug. "So why did you drag me out here? To apologize? Well, apology accepted. Now can we go back to the dance? You can make it up to me by letting the other men know they're safe to ask me to dance."

As she stepped away, he caught hold of her arm. Drawing her back, he looked down at her with a deep level of some emotion. What was it?

"Jonesy? What's wrong?"

Was he leaving sooner than he'd planned? She'd been counting on two more weeks with him.

He took her hands in his. Eva shivered.

"I've been thinking, Eva. We've been trying to be friends. But it just isn't working out."

Tears sprang to Eva's eyes. "I thought it was. I'm sorry if you don't want to be my friend."

"Eva." He let out a short laugh. "The reason it isn't working out is because I've fallen in love with you."

He pulled her closer and touched his forehead to hers. "I'm so in love with you I can't stand the thought of leaving you."

Giddy relief filled Eva. "Oh, Jonesy. Finally."

"Finally?" he whispered.

"I've loved you since the moment I met you. I thought you were going to go away and I'd never see you again."

Jonesy straightened up and lifted her hands to his lips, pressing a kiss on one and then the other. "Will you marry me?"

A smile spread across Eva's lips. "With all my heart, Jonesy."

Then he did what Eva had dreamed of since the day they'd met. He gently released her hands and gathered her around the waist. His fingers spanned her back as he pulled her closer. His head lowered.

At the first touch of his warm lips on hers, Eva's eyes closed, and she sank against him, accepting his tender kiss and responding with all the love she had to offer him. Her knees weakened as he deepened the kiss.

Disappointment flooded her when he pulled away. "Let's go back and tell our folks." His voice was husky and a bit breathless.

Eva nodded and grabbed his hand. "Ma is going to be so happy that I'm finally settling down. Only I can't imagine what all the old dowagers in town will have to talk about now. But just think. I can join their little Ladies' Aid

Society." She pinched her nose and spoke in a high tone, mimicking Mrs. Barker, the prim and proper owner of the town boardinghouse: "Because don't you know, only married women are allowed because they often discuss childbirth and other subjects unsuitable for delicate, unmarried women." Eva squeezed his hand. "But now they'll have to let me in."

She'd expected him to laugh, but he didn't. As a matter of fact, when she studied his face in the light of the bright moon, his expression appeared downright sickened. "I don't have to join the ladies' society. But I'll have to come up with a good reason to give Ma; otherwise she'll insist, and I'll give in."

"Eva, honey, stop talking for a second."

Heat rose to her cheeks. "I'm sorry, Jonesy. I thought you were just as happy and excited as I am."

"Excited? I'm ecstatic. My joy has no bounds at the thought that you love me and want to become my wife."

"Then. . ."

He gathered a shaky breath. "Eva, I still plan to move back to Texas in two weeks."

Eva's ire rose, sudden and hot. She jerked her hand from his. "Then what was all this, Jonesy? A game?"

"Of course not."

"Well, what sort of marriage do you suppose we could have if you're all the way in Texas and I'm—" She halted in midsentence as clarity struck her hard, like a tall tree crashing on top of her. "Do you mean to tell me you want me to come with you?"

"Yes."

"Oh." All of her strength sifted from her. *It hadn't been*

that long ago that she'd believed if only he'd ask her, she would follow Jonesy anywhere. But faced with the wretched reality of leaving her family, how could she possibly make such a choice?
"I—I don't know, Jonesy. How can I leave? My grammy and grandpa came west in the early days when wagon trains first brought settlers to Oregon. My pa is the only one who has ever left, and he came back. All my cousins and aunts and uncles live no farther than Oregon City, which is just a day's ride from here."

"Don't you see? This is your chance to build a life with me. You'll love Texas, Eva. There's no place on earth like it. Wild, open country."

"Apaches," Eva said flatly.

Jonesy smiled. "Not where we'd live."

"Oh, Jonesy," Eva moaned. "Isn't there any chance you might stay in Oregon? We could build a nice life here. Ranch if you want to. Or we could grow an apple orchard or even farm the way your pa does. I've heard you made a good crop. Do you know how unusual it is to bring in a good harvest the first year? You must have a knack for it."

"The land was already primed and ready for us when we got here. Mr. Winston was preparing to spend another planting and harvest season just in case the place didn't sell."

"Still. . .won't you consider it? I mean, really, what is the difference between me leaving Oregon and you deciding to stay here? Either you sacrifice or I do. Why does it have to be me?" Eva knew she sounded like a petulant child, but disappointment brought out the puerile attitude. She wanted to marry Jonesy, but she didn't want to move away.

Jonesy held her hand and pressed it against his chest. Eva

could feel the beat of his heart against the back of her hand. He spoke softly. "I've dreamed of building my own ranch since I was old enough to pull on my first pair of boots. Ranching is in my blood. Texas is in my blood. I know how to make a good living for a family there. Our family, honey. Ever since I arrived here to help Pa and Ma settle, I've counted every day, every hour almost, waiting for harvest to be over so I can go home. The only thing that has kept me from going stir-crazy has been my relationship with you. I love you, Eva. Come build a life with me in Texas. I promise you'll never regret it."

"How can you promise something like that, Jonesy?"

He stared into her eyes. "Because I'll spend every day for the rest of our lives seeing to it." He drew her close and held her.

Eva could feel his tension. "Let's go back to the dance. I need time to think."

He nodded. "I won't say anything to our parents just yet."

When they reached the edge of the crowd around the dance floor, Eva hung back. "I'm not ready to face people. W–would you mind getting me a cup of punch? I must have left mine back at the refreshment table."

A sad smile lifted the corners of his lips. "I'll be back."

Eva's insides churned as nervous energy danced through every vessel in her body. She needed to think, to pace, to move. She glanced up and saw the line of horses next to the water troughs and hitching posts. Patches stood near the end of the row, pawing the dirt as if eager to be on the move.

She'd missed her morning runs with him. Pa had forbidden them since the incident with the thieves on the road. But right now, that's just what she needed. Determination and a need to dust off some energy overrode her desire to obey her pa.

Besides, she'd be safe. The man who had almost killed her was in jail along with one of the others. They were awaiting trial, which wouldn't happen until the circuit judge came through in three months. The third man had most likely joined the rest of the horse thieves. They were probably all halfway to Mexico by now.

She was tired of being afraid. Tired of staying close to home. She and Patches needed to run. In a flash of decision, she hurried to her beloved pony and mounted him. She whipped around and left the dance.

She waited until she was out of town before she gave Patches his head. Joyous laughter exploded from her as the wind caught her hair.

❧

By the light of the moon, there was no mistaking horse and rider. He had almost given up. But there she was. This must be a sign that she belonged to him after all. He took careful aim with his pistol.

five

When Jonesy returned to the tree where he'd left Eva, she was nowhere in sight. Assuming she'd simply gone to take care of nature's call, he stood there sipping a glass of punch, holding another glass for Eva. But after fifteen minutes, his glass was empty, and he was growing concerned.

He enlisted Mrs. Riley's help, then came back to the spot beside the pine and waited for a report.

Mrs. Riley returned moments later, shaking her head. "No one's seen her." Her troubled gaze scanned the yard and the street, where the wagons and horses had thinned out quite a bit as people left for home. She touched his arm. "Jonesy! Patches is gone."

"Eva rode to the dance?"

Hope nodded. "Alongside the wagon. She was so upset about having to go alone, I didn't have the heart to forbid it. Didn't you say the two of you worked all that out?"

"Yes, ma'am. But I upset her in another way."

A smile touched her lips. "By asking her to marry you?"

"Mr. Riley told you?"

"Of course. We tell each other everything. Did she accept your proposal?"

"She was very excited, chattering on the way she does. We were headed back to the dance to tell you and Mr. Riley and my folks when we realized we didn't have the same location in mind to build our life together."

"She assumed you'd stay in Oregon."

He nodded. "And I figured she'd know I wanted her to come with me to Texas."

"Eva loves you." She said it so softly, he had to lean forward to hear it. When she spoke again, Jonesy recognized the pain in her voice. "She'll go with you. A woman in love will follow her man to the ends of the earth."

Faith that Eva might actually say yes surged through him. "Well, she might be all the way at the ends of the earth by now the way she rides that horse of hers. Let me walk you back to the party, then I'll go after her."

Mrs. Riley took his proffered arm, and they hurried back to the dance floor. "I wish she wouldn't go off alone on that wild horse of hers. But that's her pa's blood in her."

He chuckled. "Maybe I ought to put her to work around the ranch. I bet she could run down and rope a steer better than most cowhands."

"You just let her cook your meals and wash your shirts. Leave the rough riding to your men."

Jonesy grinned and tipped his hat. "Yes, ma'am."

"And when you catch up to Eva, will you take her home? Andy and I will be leaving in the next few minutes, so there's no need to bring her back here."

"Yes, ma'am."

It hadn't occurred to him that Eva might have come to the dance on Patches. Why hadn't he noticed the pony hitched up somewhere? His stomach churned as he mounted Lady Anne.

He dug his heels into the mare's flanks and urged her faster as he followed the road out of town. If he knew Eva, she'd take the road as far as her uncle Michael's property, which extended for several miles, then she'd cut across the field where she could really run Patches.

He'd definitely have to have a discussion with her about her taking off like that. Running a horse at night, even a good horse like Patches, was dangerous. She should know better.

After trotting for a few miles, Lady Anne suddenly pulled back and whinnied. A shadowy form in the road blocked their path.

Bitter panic threatened to choke Jonesy. "Eva?" he called. As he drew closer, he realized the form was too large to be a human. It looked more like. . .a horse.

Oh, Lord, is it Patches? He pulled Lady Anne to a halt and drew his pistol, then moved cautiously toward the horse.

As he came close, the light from the moon confirmed his fear. He knelt beside the pony. Patches lifted his neck, then lowered it back to the ground.

Jonesy scanned the area. Eva was nowhere to be seen. She never would have left Patches alone. She knew folks would be coming this way after the dance. If the horse had stumbled and fallen in the dark, she would have waited for someone to happen by.

Acidic fear burned in his stomach. "Eva!" He looked closely around the horse for any sign of which way Eva had gone. A smear in the dust around Patches made him bend for a closer look. Eva hadn't walked away. Someone—or something—had dragged her into the woods.

Operating on instinct, he gripped his pistol and entered the woods in the direction of the drag marks on the road. Even during the daylight hours, the woods could be dark and foreboding. Able to hide anything that didn't want to be found. How on earth was he going to find a woman who was most likely hurt and had been dragged away against her will?

Lord, he prayed, *I know You have Your eyes on Eva right now. Please lead me to her.*

"Eva!" he called out. "Eva, it's Jonesy. Where are you?" He pushed a branch away from his face. "Eva! Make some noise so I can find you, honey."

Branches and leaves crashed in front of him. In the dark woods, he could just make out a human form running in the opposite direction. He knew it couldn't be Eva. She'd never run away from him. Perhaps it was her attacker.

"Eva!" Panic rose higher. He moved through the woods with no sense of direction, just putting one foot in front of the other.

"Eva!"

Please, Lord. Please.

"Eva!"

Oh, Lord. Please. Please. Please.

He tripped with the next step, and even before he hit the ground, he realized what his foot had caught on. A human body.

Jonesy pulled himself up to his knees. When he recognized the still form, fear gripped him with an unrelenting fist. "Eva, sweetheart. Oh, please, God. Can you hear me?"

She moaned, and he thought his heart would stop.

"It'll be all right, honey." He smoothed back her hair, and his hand came away slick with blood. The thought of anyone harming his Eva made him nearly insane with anger. But more urgent was the need to get Eva to the doctor.

He lifted her in his arms. She moaned again as he stood.

His heart clenched. There was no time to see if she had any broken bones. No time to worry about whether or not movement would cause her more pain.

He buried his face in the curve of her neck. As he carried her back through the woods, tears flowed down his face.

He couldn't risk riding with her on horseback. Instead he cradled her against his chest and walked toward town, not caring if his horse became the next in a line of horse thefts. He moved with swift footfalls. His sobs were the only sound on the lonely road.

❧

Wails of agony awakened Eva from deep, nightmarish unconsciousness. When the pain hit her full force, she realized the wails were coming from her own throat. She forced herself to be silent and tried to make sense of the pain. The darkness. Searing pain stabbed her sides, her head, her leg.

A moan escaped her lips.

A door creaked open.

"Wh–who is it?" Darkness engulfed her as if she were entering a cave without a candle.

Ma's soft voice reached into the darkness. "Darling, it's all right. You're safe." Gentle hands took hers between them.

"Ma?"

"Yes, Eva, it's me."

"Why can't I see anything?"

"Your eyes are swollen shut. But Doc Smith says you'll be able to open them soon." Her voice caught in her throat, and Eva could tell she was fighting to keep from breaking down. "I'm so glad you're finally awake. I'm going to send Pa to town. Doc said to let him know the second you woke up."

Panic gripped her. Eva made a grab for Ma's hands before

she could take away their warmth. "No, wait, Ma. P–please don't leave me."

"All right, darling. We'll wait until Pa comes in from his shop. Then he can go get the doc."

Relief that she wasn't to be left alone in the dark flooded her. "What happened to me?"

"You don't remember?"

Eva shook her head. "Not entirely." She'd been riding Patches at a run when all of a sudden a shot rang out. Patches fell, and she hit her head. She gasped. "Patches. Is he all right? I remember hearing a gunshot. Did someone shoot Patches?"

"Yes, darling, but it's only a little wound in one of his hind legs. His running-wild days might be over, but he'll live. He's in the barn getting fat on oats."

Eva nearly wept with relief, but the swelling of her eyes kept tears at bay. "I don't understand, Ma. Who would want to shoot Patches?"

Feeling a thick wall of hesitation, Eva squeezed her mother's hand. "It's all right. I need to know."

Ma's breath came in shaky bursts. "Eva. A man dragged you into the woods. He beat you and. . ."

Eva's throat went dry. Horror slashed through her mind as more clarity returned. She remembered being dragged through the woods. She remembered. . . . *Oh, dear God.* She remembered it all.

"Ma!" Her own shrill voice sounded foreign. She pressed her hands against her ears.

"I'm sorry, my darling. I'm so sorry." Ma's arms surrounded Eva. But no comfort came this time. In fact, Eva felt nothing as she rested her head against her mother's shoulder.

"What all is wrong with me?" she asked in a flat tone.

Ma pulled back. "Several broken ribs. Your leg is sprained. The doctor thinks that happened when Patches fell. You've been unconscious for four days, so Doc Smith wasn't sure about the extent of your head injury. But praise the Lord, it appears you'll be fine. No memory loss or brain damage that would have kept you unconscious forever, which is what he'd feared."

Hearing her ma use the term "praise the Lord" brought an anger to Eva that she had no idea was possible to feel. Praise the Lord that she'd been beaten but not killed? How much better if she'd never been found. She surely would have died.

"Jonesy found me, didn't he?"

"Yes. As soon as he realized you'd left the dance. He walked three miles carrying you back to town before your pa and I happened upon him. That man loves you with every ounce of his being. He'll be so relieved to know you've come to. He's been here every day. As a matter of fact, I expect him anytime."

"Ma, no."

"No what?"

"I don't want to see him."

"Oh, Eva. Jonesy doesn't blame you for what that man did to you."

Deep, soul-crushing pain nearly pushed the breath from her body, leaving her an empty, nonbreathing shell. Dead. That's what she should be. She'd known she was going to die that night. Had wanted to die. And then she'd heard Jonesy's voice calling to her. Her eyes burned with tears that had no way to escape.

"I don't ever want to see him again."

"Eva, give yourself a few days to adjust. You'll feel differently."

"What good will a few days do? Will my eyesight erase the fact that I am not fit to be a wife for a good man like Jonesy?"

Eva heard a soft gasp escape her mother's lips. "Eva. That is not true. Of course you're fit to be a wife. No one thinks any of this was your fault."

"But it was. I knew better than to ride off like that. But I did it anyway. I might as well have offered myself to that man."

"Don't talk like that." Ma's tone was harsh with shock and distress. "You are as pure in the eyes of the Lord as you were before this wicked, horrible thing happened to you, darling. Jonesy knows that."

"Oh, Mother, please." Eva turned toward the window. She knew light must be shining through. If Pa was still working, nightfall hadn't arrived. Still, darkness surrounded her. Deep, all-consuming darkness that invaded her soul.

Ma's hand rubbed along her leg. Eva's skin crawled, and she had to fight the urge not to shake her off. Even that small touch caused her pain. Not physical, but another kind of pain, one she couldn't identify. But she knew something was different inside her.

It was fear. She'd never been afraid.

"Eva, believe me. Jonesy loves you."

Eva gave a short, bitter laugh. "He would never take back his proposal. But you can be sure he's been praying every night that I won't wake up or, if I do, that I'll let him out of it by refusing him."

"Eva Riley. You know Jonesy better than that."

Ignoring her ma's interruption, Eva continued her thought as though she'd never spoken. "Since I've obviously awakened, I'm going to have to give him the second option. I'll just have to refuse to marry him and send him on to Texas without me."

"Don't make rash decisions after the ordeal you've been through. Take some time to think about it."

"My mind is made up. I don't want to see him. If you love me, please respect my wishes. I don't want to see Jonesy." She winced as pain stabbed her head.

"We won't talk about this for now. You're in too much pain to think clearly. Dr. Smith left some laudanum for you, but I'm not sure you should have any until he examines you."

"Please, Ma. The pain is unbearable."

"All right. I'll give you less than he suggested. That should still help some."

Ma left and returned a moment later. She spooned the bitter liquid between Eva's swollen lips. "There you go, darling. You get some rest now."

"Stay with me until I fall asleep?"

Ma patted Eva's hand. "I'll be right next to your bed in that chair."

Almost immediately Eva grew drowsy. Despite her inability to see past her swollen eyes, in her mind she couldn't escape the vivid images of her brutal attack. She welcomed the approaching sleep.

Perhaps this time she wouldn't wake up.

six

"What do you mean, she won't see me?" Hurt slashed at Jonesy as he stood on the Rileys' porch, staring into Andy's brown eyes. Eyes so like Eva's.

"Give her some time, son. She's been through quite an ordeal."

"With all due respect, sir, I know what she's been through." Jonesy released a frustrated breath. "I want to be there for her. To help her get well. Why doesn't she want to see me?"

"Shame, most likely. You don't understand what something like this does to a woman."

"I want to understand, Mr. Riley. I want Eva to lean on me. I want to take her away from the memories. I'll postpone my trip until spring to give her time to heal. Will you tell her that for me? I can't bear the thought of living the rest of my life without her."

He'd been so close to marrying her. They should be celebrating. Making plans to travel to Texas. Oh, sure, she hadn't agreed to marry him yet. Well, he supposed she had accepted his proposal, but he was fully aware she'd only done so assuming they'd remain in Oregon. Regardless, he felt sure she would have eventually come around to his way of thinking. "On second thought, I should be the one to tell her I still want to marry her. If she hears my voice, she'll know I'm being honest."

"You're a decent man, Jonesy. And I know you love my

daughter as deeply as I love her mother."

"Then please," Jonesy pleaded, "let me see her."

Andy shook his head. "I'm sorry. But I can't go against her wishes in this."

Dejected, Jonesy turned away and mounted Lady Anne. The most frustrating thing in the world to him was that his Eva lay in that bed day after day, hurting physically and emotionally, and he could do nothing to ease her pain. He wanted to hold her, to reassure her. To let his gentle touch soothe away the memories of violence and pain.

As he rode away, helpless fury overtook him. He turned the mare in the direction of town. His throat clogged when he reached the spot on the road where Eva had been accosted, dragged into the woods, violated. Tears burned his eyes.

With single-minded purpose, he guided Lady Anne forward toward town, his mind repeatedly replaying the sight of his beloved Eva when he'd found her.

He halted the horse in front of the sheriff's office and dismounted.

Billy stood up when he entered. "I expected you a few days ago."

Surprise lifted Jonesy's brow. "You did?"

"Yep. I figured you'd be looking for some answers from those two vermin." He jerked his thumb toward the back room, which was divided into four jail cells.

"Have you questioned them?"

He nodded. "Even tried to cut a deal with them."

"What kind of a deal?"

"Let one of them go for information on where the others went."

"How will that help us find the man who hurt Eva?"

"I figure he was the fellow who got away. He's most likely fled the area. And unless I miss my guess, he's headed straight to the camp where the others are hiding out with Mr. Compton's horses.

Jonesy nodded. "That makes sense."

"The big guy in there says the man who got away has done the same thing to other women. None of the others lived."

This was all his fault. He should have paid closer attention. If only he could go back and change things.

"So you offered to let one of them go in exchange for information on the rest of the gang's whereabouts?"

Billy nodded. "I didn't figure they'd go for the deal. I mean, what good would it do to lead me to the hideout? I'd still arrest them for horse thieving."

"Can I talk to them?"

"I suppose I can give you a few minutes alone with them. Leave your gun on my desk."

An idea formed in Jonesy's mind as he walked from Billy's office to the room that housed the cells.

The only occupants were the two horse thieves. The older man was stretched out on a bench, one enormous arm flung across his forehead, covering his eyes.

The younger one gave him a shove when he saw Jonesy. "Hey, Randy," he whispered. "Wake up. We got company."

"What?" Randy snorted and sat up. He smoothed back his unruly gray hair. A sneer twisted his nasty, half-toothless mouth. "What do you want?"

Jonesy grabbed the wooden chair sitting against the wall opposite the cells. He carried it forward about three feet from the bars and straddled the seat, resting his forearms on the back of the chair, facing the outlaws. "I'm here to offer you a deal."

Randy let out a humorless chuckle. "Save it. Your sheriff already tried to make a deal. Problem is, he gets unfair advantage, and we'd just get caught again."

Jonesy inclined his head. "I agree that was a bad deal for you. You're too smart to be fooled by some lawman who wants to make a name for himself in this part of the country."

Randy's eyes narrowed. "What could you offer that's any different? You ain't even a deputy."

Jonesy leaned closer. "Keep your voice down. I don't want the sheriff to hear this."

"What is it?" The younger fellow had *stupid* written all over his face. His mouth hung half open, and his eyes were round with curiosity.

"Hush up, Timothy. I'm askin' the questions." Randy took a swipe at him with the palm of his hand. Timothy ducked out of his way. Maybe he wasn't quite as dumb as he looked.

Jonesy spoke in low tones. "I'll get you both out of here if you'll take me to the man who hurt Eva."

A scowl creased Randy's wide face. "That's the same thing the sheriff offered. I said no to him, and I'm sayin' no to you."

Jonesy returned his frown. He was in no mood to be turned down by a couple of thugs with no other options but hanging. "What I'm offering isn't the same deal."

"Oh yeah? How's yours different?"

Jonesy shrugged and kept a steady eye on the criminal in order to gauge his reaction. "I'm not talking about releasing you legally. I could break you out."

Young Timothy laughed and nudged Randy. "That does sound different, don't it, boss?"

"It's a trick, you idiot."

"If you don't take me up on my offer, then you're the idiot." Jonesy glanced cautiously toward the door, then back to the outlaws.

"So what's in it for us?"

"Freedom, pure and simple. The punishment for horse thieving is hanging. You have one chance to get out of this cell, and that's by agreeing to my plan."

"How do we know you won't lead the sheriff straight to us?"

"After he figures out that I've let you escape and that I'm with you, I'm going to be a wanted man, as well."

"He's got a point there," Timothy said.

Randy nodded thoughtfully, ignoring his companion's enthusiastic response. "Then why would you take the chance?"

"As long as I get the man who hurt Eva," Jonesy said with fervor, "I'll sit in jail for however long I have to."

"Let's say I agree to this." He raised his eyebrow. "And I ain't sayin' I am. But just supposin'. . ."

Jonesy's heart increased in rhythm, and he fought to keep the eagerness from his voice. "All right. Supposing."

"How do you plan on breaking us out?"

"Easy. Billy is escorting a certain young lady to a town musicale tonight. He'll be gone for two hours, and most of the town will be at the meeting hall."

"The sheriff'll most likely take the keys with him," Randy pointed out, stroking his stubbled jaw.

"I know where the spare set is. We've been friends for months. And his sister is my bride-to-be."

"You mean the one that Pete—"

"Yes," Jonesy broke in. "So do we have a deal?"

"You're just going to walk in and let us out?"

Jonesy regarded him with a grim smile. "You'll have to keep your wrists tied. I don't intend to have my throat slit."

"What's to stop you from slicing mine?"

"I'm not after you. I'm after your friend. You lead me to him, and I don't care what you do. Until then, you'll have to stay tied up."

"All right. We'll do it your way. It's less than a day's ride, unless they got tired of waiting and left without us."

Timothy's eyes grew wide. "You don't think they did, do you? Sam owes me four dollars for that last ranch we—"

"Shut up, Timothy."

Jonesy smirked. "I don't care about all that. I only care about getting the man who hurt the woman I plan to marry."

❧

Eva stared toward the light. It had been two days since she'd awakened, and she was just beginning to see images and light through the slits in her eyes. The swelling had receded enough to allow little slices of vision. For that, she was grateful.

Fear had taken hold of almost every waking minute as her imagination took her to the dark, shadowed corners of her mind. Horrific memories came back with such startling detail that often she shook in her bed. The man had wanted her dead. Had said angry things that made no sense, as though he were her husband and she had been unfaithful.

She jumped when the door opened. "Who is it?"

"It's only me, darling." Ma's presence afforded Eva small moments of peace. They only lasted as long as she was in the room and only if she didn't speak of that night or of Jonesy.

"I've brought you some leftover chicken pie from last night's supper."

"Thank you, Ma. I am a little hungry."

The painful process of sitting up left Eva breathless. Ma set the plate in her hands and handed her a napkin. "You can see a little better today?"

Eva nodded. "A little."

Ma sat on the chair next to the bed, rustling pages. She read the Bible to her four times a day. At breakfast, lunch, supper, and bedtime. Eva had tried to dissuade her, but this was not something on which Hope Riley was willing to compromise. Resolve flowed over Eva. No sense in fighting it.

"Today we read from Psalm 118. 'O give thanks unto the Lord; for he is good: because his mercy endureth for ever. Let Israel now say, that his mercy endureth for ever. Let the house of Aaron now say, that his mercy endureth for ever. Let them now that fear the Lord say, that his mercy endureth for ever. I called upon the Lord in distress: the Lord answered me, and set me in a large place. The Lord is on my side; I will not fear: what can man do unto me?' "

Eva gave a short laugh. "What indeed?"

Ma's silence filled the room.

"Well?" Eva asked, hearing the anger in her own voice. "Don't you see my point?"

"Yes, darling. But sometimes bad things happen to good

people due to the wickedness of mankind. That has nothing to do with the goodness of God."

"Then why does God promise protection? Why does He say angels will guard us? Why even pretend to be God if He can't keep us safe? Or if He can, why didn't He?"

The shaking of Eva's faith over the past few days had left her feeling emptier than she'd felt in her entire life. Since childhood, she'd known that God was almighty, sovereign, omnipotent. She'd felt securely tucked in the cocoon of her sheltered life and her large, protective family. She hadn't needed to question her faith, because she'd never faced any real ordeals. Until now. And now she knew that God wasn't who He claimed to be.

Bitterness seeped around purity until her innocence was all but gone. Smothered by hatred.

"What if I ask Greg to come and speak with you? You might find comfort in confiding in a parson."

"No thank you, Ma. I'm not interested."

"Oh, honey. Don't turn your heart away from Jesus. He's the only One who can get you through this time of sorrow and pain."

"I didn't turn away from Him, Ma. He turned away from me."

seven

Rain beat down without mercy on Jonesy and the two men as they set out at dusk. Getting the two out of the jail unnoticed couldn't have been easier. Between the musicale and the drenching rain, not many people ventured out. And those who did weren't interested in three men riding away from town. Jonesy had brought two extra horses from home. He'd unlocked the cell and walked them out the front door without a lick of trouble.

"Look here, mister," Randy whined. "You're gonna have to untie us, or we ain't gonna be able to make it through this mud. My horse is about to toss me off."

Jonesy glanced at Timothy, who appeared to be having no trouble at all with his mount. Randy was obviously faking it.

Jonesy knew better than to untie the men. If he was going to meet up with the man who had violated Eva and make sure he got what he deserved, he had to keep the upper hand with these two—especially Randy. "If you fall off the horse, you'll walk."

"You ain't got no heart, do ya?" But he sat up straighter in the saddle and stopped struggling, just as Jonesy had suspected he would.

By the time they'd ridden for two hours, the rain had stopped, the clouds had rolled back, and a bright moon lit their path. Jonesy allowed no stops. For any reason. The men rode in silence, listening to the occasional sounds of wolves howling in the distance, the hooting of owls, the horses' hooves pounding the trail.

When the morning sun broke through ahead of them, Jonesy remembered the morning he'd met Eva. Her indignation at falling in the river. Her smile that lit the morning like the dawn.

Then the memory of her battered body ripped through him.

"How much farther?" Jonesy's tone was gruff, leaving no room for foolishness.

"A couple hours," Randy replied. He gave a short, humorless laugh. "You know, my gang ain't gonna let you just walk outta there with one of our own."

"I don't need them to let me do anything," Jonesy growled. "If I'm holding a gun to their leader's head, they'll hand him over."

"Why are you doin' this, anyway? It's just a woman. Plenty more where she came from."

Timothy snorted. "Yeah, plenty more."

Repulsed, Jonesy kept his thoughts to himself. Why was he going to all this trouble to find the man who had hurt Eva? *Simple.* The only way she would ever be free was if she knew the man would not be coming back.

Besides, that horrible creature had to be punished for what he had done.

And according to Mr. and Mrs. Riley, Eva was ashamed. Tears of mercy threatened to spill over. How could she believe she was to blame for anything that had happened to her?

Randy's grating voice cut through his musings. "Cat got your tongue?"

"Shut up. My reasons are my own. Besides, someone like

you would never understand."

"What do you mean by that? I ain't good enough?"

"No, you're not."

Randy didn't respond.

Jonesy's conscience pricked him. He knew every hair on Randy's head was numbered by the God of love and grace. Despite the contempt Jonesy felt for the man, he knew God loved him.

"Maybe you just never had a chance to be the kind of person you were meant to be, Randy. I don't know." The offering cost him. He had no desire to be anything but brutal to this man. Even if he wasn't the one who did the ultimate damage to Eva, Randy had been about to slice her throat and steal her horse the day he'd come upon them on the road. He was no better than the rapist. "Any man who could hurt Eva doesn't know the kind of love I have for her."

"I loved a woman once," Randy replied in his defense.

Jonesy doubted it. Still, they had a long ride ahead of them, so why not play along to pass the time? Timothy seemed to be far away somewhere in his mind. "If you really loved someone, tell me about her."

"I ain't telling you nothin' about nobody."

"Have it your way."

Randy turned in his saddle and stared at Jonesy. The man's frown cut deep grooves between his eyes. "She was nice to me."

"And that made you fall in love with her?"

"Yep."

"What was her name?"

"Cynthia. Her pa was the town preacher."

"Really?" Jonesy hadn't meant to say the word out loud,

but he'd expected Randy to say the woman was a saloon girl who had to be nice to him as part of her job.

Apparently offended by Jonesy's surprised tone, Randy snorted. "You don't think I can fall for a good girl?"

"I guess you could. But what good girl would return your feelings?"

"If you're goin' to insult me, just forget the whole thing."

With a shrug, Jonesy let it go. After a minute or two, Randy resumed the conversation as though he'd never been offended.

"It was my first time in jail. I was young and not so fat. The ladies seemed to have a thing for me." He grinned.

Jonesy was hard pressed not to spit. "I'm sure they did." In Randy's mind, maybe. "So how did an outlaw meet a pretty preacher's daughter?"

"Her ma fixed supper for the prisoners, even though she had a big family of her own to feed. Cynthia was the oldest of ten young'uns. One day when her mama was laid up having a baby, she came in to give us our food. The sheriff was busy, so she had to bring us our basket herself." He drew a sharp breath as though reliving the memory. "She didn't shy away from me like most other respectable women."

"I can understand why you took a shine to her."

"You don't know the half of it. She was the most beautiful thing I'd ever seen. Her hair was like corn silk. When she handed me a plate, she looked right into my eyes and smiled."

"So maybe she wasn't such a good girl after all?"

A growl crawled from Randy's throat. "I don't like your tone."

"Well, I don't like that you almost killed Eva."

Randy's eyes took on a reflective stare. Jonesy's statement had apparently hit home.

"What happened with Cynthia?"

A breath lifted Randy's shoulders. "Her ma was laid up for quite a spell, so Cynthia brought the food every day."

"The sheriff allowed a young woman to bring dinner to a bunch of thieves?"

"More than that. He let her stay and talk to me. She brought her Bible and read out of the Good Book."

"Ah, so the jail was Cynthia's mission field."

"I guess. But it was more than that between her and me."

Apparently Randy really had cared for someone.

"Since I was just the lookout and didn't hurt anyone or steal anything, I got out before the rest of them."

"So then you started courting Cynthia, I guess?" Jonesy said it flippantly, sarcastically. No respectable family would allow an outlaw to court the town sweetheart and preacher's daughter.

But the sarcasm seemed lost on Randy. "Her pa offered me the barn loft to sleep in, for good honest labor. I didn't care too much for farmwork, but I'd have done anything to be near Cynthia."

Jonesy understood that feeling.

"I went to church regular-like with her family and finally understood about Jesus."

The holy name coming from this outlaw's mouth shot through Jonesy like an arrow piercing his heart. How could a man like Randy know Jesus?

His face softened. "Shortly after that, I married her."

"Married?" Jonesy hadn't expected that. "What happened?"

"She died just three months later. Snakebite." He sniffed,

then cleared his throat. "She had just told me we were going to have a baby."

"I'm truly sorry, Randy."

"She wanted to name him Luke, after my pa."

"Maybe you do know how I feel about Eva, then. Think about Cynthia next time you or one of your pals is about to rape a woman."

Anger flashed in the black eyes. "I ain't never done anything of the sort. And I wouldn't have let Pete do it if I hadn't been locked up in here. So it's your own fault that happened to your girl. If I hadn't been in jail, he wouldn't have done it."

Anger boiled Jonesy's blood. This man had the nerve to blame him? "If I hadn't stopped you that day, Eva would be dead. So don't pretend you're any better than Pete." The name of Eva's attacker tasted foul in Jonesy's mouth. He spat on the ground.

A loud snort from Timothy diverted their attention. He jerked his head up. "Are we almost there?"

"Boy," Randy said with disgust, "were you sleeping?"

"I guess so." He gave a sheepish grin. "Ma always says I kin sleep just about anywheres."

Jonesy shook his head and retreated to his own thoughts. He didn't want to hear about these outlaws' mothers. It was bad enough that he now saw Randy as more than a thug. The man obviously suffered from deep inner wounds. If Cynthia hadn't died, Randy would probably be a respectable farmer with a wife and a crop of children by now.

Bitterness, anger, and unforgiveness could blacken any man's soul. That's why Jonesy had to bring Eva's attacker to justice. Give her a chance to heal. Then the forgiveness could begin.

He looked at Randy, a big, brawny man with blood on his hands and the end of a rope facing him someday. A man who had loved so deeply he couldn't bear the loss. As Jonesy watched Randy's slumped shoulders, he thanked God for grace.

❧

When Eva opened her eyes, the first thing she noticed was that she could actually see the morning sun shining through the bedroom window. She squinted against the brightness she'd been unable to see for the past few days.

Having her sight restored raised her spirits considerably. She'd ask Ma to have Lily pick out some new dime novels so she would have something to help pass the time. Maybe she'd even ask for a book of poetry. Jonesy had forced her to listen to it so much, she'd actually grown fond of Lord Byron.

Jonesy. Eva's heart picked up a few beats as his image flickered in her mind. She would have been planning a wedding right now if. . .

If only. . .

❧

"There."

Jonesy jerked his head up at the sound of Randy's voice. The first words between them for two hours.

"In that cliff. There's a cave."

"You have horses in a cave?"

"That's where we brand them. Every couple of days, one of us takes two horses and heads to Oregon City to sell them."

"I'm supposed to believe you're going to give me that information just like that?"

"Don't matter none anyway. You ain't gonna make it out of this alive."

"I will."

"We'll see."

Jonesy cautiously rode a couple of miles more until they reached the bottom of the cliff. Then he dismounted and lifted his pistol from his holster. He grabbed his extra rope and nodded at Timothy. "Get down."

Timothy unlooped his bound wrists from the pommel of his saddle and dismounted.

"Over there," Jonesy said, pointing the barrel of his pistol to a tree. "Sit down."

"What are you gonna do?"

"I only need one prisoner. And I have a feeling your friend is more important to the rest of your gang than you are."

Timothy sat still while Jonesy tied him to the tree, then took the boy's handkerchief from his pocket and tied it through his mouth. "Sorry, but I can't have you calling out a warning."

Jonesy looked up warily at Randy. Standing a safe distance from the horse, he nodded to the outlaw. "Your turn. Get down."

Randy dismounted awkwardly. Jonesy regretted that he couldn't gag Randy, too, but he didn't want to holster his pistol with the man's powerful legs still free.

"All right," Jonesy said. "Let's go. Slow. And don't try anything. As soon as I have Pete, I won't try to hold you."

He glanced down at Timothy. "You'll be all right. They'll come and untie you as soon as I'm gone."

Timothy's eyes widened, but his focus went over Jonesy's shoulder.

"Drop the gun."

Dread clenched Jonesy's gut at the unfamiliar voice. He turned slowly. Two men stood holding guns on him. One, who looked identical to Timothy, was wearing a pair of buckskin chaps and a ripped calico shirt.

Jonesy knew better than to try anything stupid. He tossed his pistol forward.

"Good to see you, Al," Randy said, a chuckle rumbling in his barrel chest. "This fool thought he'd walk outta here with Pete."

"Pete?" The redhead kept his rifle on Jonesy but turned to Randy. "We thought he was with you."

"What do you mean?" asked Jonesy.

Al sneered and backhanded him hard across the jaw. "Shut up." He nodded to the redhead. "Untie Randy and your dim-witted brother."

"This feller's girl got attacked," Randy said while Timothy's brother dismounted. "We figured Pete did it and ran off to find you."

"Pete got another one?" Anger marred Al's brow. "You know what I told him after the last one."

Randy nodded. "Guess that's why he didn't come lookin' for you. We probably ain't gonna see him again."

Panic seized Jonesy. "You mean to tell me Pete's not here?"

Al glared. "I told you to shut yer mouth."

Jonesy glared at Randy. "We had a deal."

"I kept my part of the bargain. I brung you to the gang, didn't I?"

"You knew Pete wouldn't be here. I'm a day away from Eva, and that monster could still be around Hobbs. How am I going to protect her?"

"That ain't our problem, mister," Al broke in.

Jonesy kept his focus on Randy. "Wouldn't you have given anything to keep Cynthia safe?"

Randy's face reddened, and his eyes flashed in anger. "Shut up about her."

"What if someone like Pete had snuck around watching her for two weeks and then violated her? Almost killed her?"

"Shut up!" Randy stepped forward until they were nose to nose, his rancid breath nearly choking Jonesy.

"Enough of this," Al barked. "We're pulling out with the last two horses tonight. And we ain't takin' an extra man, so move outta the way."

His words sliced through Jonesy like an ax head, but he refused to be deterred. "Think about it, Randy."

"Cynthia died a long time ago." He nodded toward Al and the twins. "This is all the family I got left. If I turn against them, I'm alone."

"Turn against us?" Al frowned. "You thinking about being a turncoat?"

"No."

"Then let's get it done." Al handed him a knife. "Use this. We don't want to make any noise."

Jonesy saw hesitation mar Randy's expression. He jumped on it. "Randy, what would Cynthia want you to do?"

The second the words left his lips, Randy's face darkened. He approached with utter hatred flashing in his eyes. "I told you not to talk about her anymore. I'm done remembering."

Randy raised the knife to Jonesy's throat.

He returned the man's murderous gaze with unflinching dignity, though everything in him screamed to beg for his life.

A blast of gunfire sounded. The twins dove for cover.

Randy landed with a thud on the ground. He clapped his hand to a bleeding shoulder and looked up at Jonesy with accusing eyes. "You double-crossed me."

Jonesy glanced at the sheriff, who had been following them since they left Hobbs, then turned back to Randy. "Now we're even."

Al dropped with the next blast from Billy's gun.

Jonesy dove for his pistol, which the outlaws hadn't bothered to retrieve from where he'd dropped it.

When his fingers were inches away from the gun, Jonesy felt a sharp pain slice through his leg. Crying out, he looked down. Randy pulled the knife out and raised it again. In a split second, Jonesy kicked with his other leg and knocked the knife from Randy's hand. Randy rolled to his feet and ran for the nearest horse.

Despite another round of fire, Randy rode away amid a cloud of dust. Jonesy crawled to cover and snatched his handkerchief from his pocket. His leg throbbed, and blood poured from the knife wound in his calf.

"Jonesy," Billy called. "You okay?"

"I'll live."

"How many more are there?"

"Just two, and neither of them seem that smart. We won't have any trouble bringing them in. It's dead or alive, right?"

"That's right. And I brought along plenty of bullets, so I'll outlast them."

"Wait!"

Jonesy recognized Timothy's voice.

"Don't shoot. We're coming out."

"Do it, then," Billy said. "Slowly, with both hands in the air. Any sudden moves, and I'll open fire."

Within moments, Billy had both of the red-haired men tied up. He glanced at Jonesy. "You going to make it back home?"

"I'll have to."

Billy nodded. "Which one is Pete?"

"Neither." Jonesy flinched against the pain in his leg as he limped to his horse. "Apparently this isn't the first time he's done something like this. Even these vermin didn't care for it. They had told him not to do it again. That's why he didn't come back to them."

Billy's face blanched. "You mean he could still be in town?"

Jonesy gave a grim nod. "Or close by."

They slung Al's lifeless body over one of the horses. Once the others were mounted, they headed toward Hobbs.

eight

Though she had awakened this morning with optimism, now, mere hours later, depression clouded over Eva as she scooted beneath the blue coverlet, ready for sleep. Darkness had fallen, and Jonesy hadn't come by today. Even though she had no intention of seeing him, the fact that he had given up disappointed her.

It had only been a few days. But she supposed he had to start making his plans to go back to Texas. After all, his land meant more to him than anything.

She had told him to leave, she reasoned, so it wasn't fair to be angry with him for giving up. Still, he hadn't tried for long.

A heavy cloud hung over her, and she thrashed about as sleep eluded her. Only the darkness, and fear of what might be there if she left the safety of her bed, prevented her from throwing off the covers and pacing away the nervous energy buzzing in her stomach.

Where was Jonesy now? Was he still at home? Had he finally taken her hint yesterday and left for Texas?

In a fit of frustration, Eva labored to sit up. She glanced about the dark room, lighted only faintly by the moon shining through the window.

Her heart was racing by the time her back rested against the feather pillows propped against the headboard. A scratching noise by the window caught her attention. She tensed, fear gripping her tighter than a corset. Paralyzed, she watched as a shadow passed by, stopped, and came back. She wanted to scream, to cry out, but her throat tightened.

Then she remembered the words her attacker had whispered that awful night: *This ain't over.*

The screams found their voice. Eva couldn't stop even when Pa and Ma burst through the door.

"What is it, Little Papoose?" Pa took Eva into his arms, and the screams gave way to silent sobs.

"He came back for me, Pa. Just like he said he would."

"What do you mean?"

"I saw him outside the window."

"Oh, honey, you must have been dreaming," Ma said. "That evil man is gone. As a matter of fact, Jonesy and Billy tricked those other two outlaws into leading them right to the hideout for the whole gang of thieves and cutthroats. So you don't have anything to worry about."

"Hope," Pa said, his voice ringing with frustration, "Billy told me that in confidence. Eva wasn't supposed to know about this until it was all over."

"Jonesy went after the outlaws?" Eva asked.

Pa patted her leg and stood. "I'll go have a look around outside."

"No!" Palpable fear slithered up from Eva's gut until she felt it in her chest and in her throat. "You can't go outside. What if he's still out there?"

"I've survived a lot of things in my day. I'll be careful." He leaned over and kissed her forehead. "Don't worry. I'll be right back."

With foreboding, Eva watched him leave.

Ma took Pa's seat on the bed next to her. "It'll be all right, Eva. I'm sure you were only dreaming."

"No, I wasn't, Ma." Eva pulled away. "I know what I saw."

Ma's eyes flashed hurt, and guilt pricked Eva. But she had to be heard.

"I couldn't sleep, so I sat up. And when I looked over to the window, I saw him walking back and forth. Then he tried to get inside." Ma still didn't look convinced. Eva sat up slightly and patted her pillows. "Mama, look! Why would my pillows be propped up if I had been sleeping?"

For the first time, a worried frown creased her mother's brow. A light glowed outside the window where Pa held the lantern.

"Eva, darling. What did you mean when you said that he came back for you like he promised?"

Swallowing hard, Eva fought the image. "I was barely conscious, Ma. But when Jonesy started calling my name, that scared him. Before he ran away, he said he'd be back. He kept saying I had betrayed him. But the only time I've ever seen him was that day on the road. He must have mistaken me for someone else. I kept thinking he'd realize I wasn't the woman he thought I was and he'd stop. But he didn't."

"Oh, Eva. You've been through so much." Hope put her arms around her daughter. But Eva stayed limp, unmoving. Surprisingly, for the first time since thinking or talking about that night, there were no tears. She was just so tired.

"Jesus, heal her."

Ma's prayer was cut short when Pa came back into the room carrying several boards and a hammer. Eva searched his eyes, and terror cut a line through her heart. "I was right, wasn't I?"

He gave a grim nod. "Someone was out there, all right. I looked around and couldn't find any signs that he might still be here. But I'm not taking any chances that he might come back."

Pa made an imposing figure when he was determined. Eva had always been a little in awe of him. Spending his young adult years as a wagon scout, meeting Indians. He'd even married an Indian girl who had died before he met Eva's ma. His wild spirit had always reached out to Eva. Had always inspired her. How her cowardice must disappoint him.

He glanced at Ma over his shoulder. "Hope, will you come hold the other end of the board?"

Ma stood immediately and went to him.

Eva watched her parents close her in, nailing boards over her window as though she were a princess in a tower. Keeping her locked away and safe from the dangers of the big, bad world.

Though part of her enjoyed the safety those boards afforded, another part of her deeply resented the confinement. Now there was nothing for her to see but the inside of this room. No light shining through, no birds flying by.

"That ought to do it." He walked across the room. "If you hear one sound, you be sure to call out. We're going to leave your bedroom door open."

Eva's heart picked up speed.

Pa studied her face. "I'll spend the night in the chair. Don't worry, honey."

"I'm sorry, Pa."

Setting his hammer on the table next to the bed, he sat beside her. "For what?"

"For being so afraid."

"No need to be sorry. It's a pa's job to keep his little girl safe."

"But I'm not a little girl anymore."

"You're my little girl. And I'll sit next to your bed as long as it takes for you to feel safe again. Until then, just know that your family loves you."

"Thank you, Pa."

He started to say something else but hesitated.

Eva smiled. "I know. You want to tell me that Jonesy loves me."

Pa gave a soft chuckle. "You know your pa pretty well, don't you?"

"Yes. We're alike in so many ways."

Ma moved softly across the room toward the bed. "I'll leave the two of you alone." She bent forward, and Eva caught the scent of apple blossoms that always seemed to cling to Ma.

She pressed a soft kiss to Eva's forehead. "Good night, darling."

"Good night, Ma."

Eva had grown increasingly short-tempered with her ma over the past few days. Not that she'd be openly disrespectful, but inside, she wanted to tell her to stop trying so hard to make her feel better. Stop feeding her cookies and cake and chicken pie, even though it was her favorite meal. Stop asking her to get out of bed and take a bath. Didn't Ma realize that no matter how many baths she took, she'd never feel clean again?

After Ma left the room, Pa picked up the Bible on the nightstand.

Eva groaned. "Oh, Pa. Do we have to read tonight? Can't we just talk?"

She received a stern glance in response. "You got something against the Bible all of a sudden, Eva?"

"No. But we haven't just talked together since. . ." Eva dropped her gaze to her fingers, twisting the covers until her knuckles grew white.

"Eva." Pa leaned forward and covered her hands with one massive paw. "No amount of talking about the weather, or how the furniture making is going, will help your soul break free from the pain."

"Oh, Pa. I'm the one who has to live with the memories. Can't I just try to live with them my own way?"

"By staying in bed? Not bathing? Turning your back on God? Honey, He's the only One who knows how you feel."

"All right, Pa." Eva closed her eyes. "Go ahead and read."

Pages rattled, then Pa's baritone voice began to read. "The Lord is my shepherd; I shall not want."

Eva felt a strange comfort in the psalm. Peace drifted over her, and the image of a gently flowing stream filled her mind as Pa read. "He leadeth me beside the still waters. He restoreth my soul." In that place between awake and asleep, Eva was aware of Pa finishing the psalm, then moving carefully to the chair next to her bed.

She drifted to sleep, feeling safe for the first time in days.

❧

Jonesy limped up the steps to the Riley home, determined that this time they weren't going to keep him from seeing Eva. It had been a full week since he'd gotten home from his useless trip to the outlaw hideout, and he had been forced to sit in bed half of that time due to the knife wound in his leg. Dr. Smith had told him he must have an angel watching over him, because if the knife had hit an inch higher, it would have tapped an artery behind his knee and he would have bled to death in a matter of minutes.

Jonesy had come out yesterday. But Mr. Riley had met him at the door. The day before, Mrs. Riley had met him. Each had the same message from Eva: "Go to Texas and forget about me."

Today he'd been smart. He'd gone to town and asked Lily to come out with him. Eva would see Lily, and he would wait on the porch, hoping her friend could convince her. If she still didn't let him in, he'd try something else tomorrow.

"I still don't think this is going to work, Jonesy," the pretty, petite blonde said, nervously patting her hair and smoothing her gown. "Even if they let me in, that doesn't mean Eva's going to see you."

"I know." He knocked on the front door.

Soon Mrs. Riley appeared. She gave him an indulgent smile. "I'll say one thing for you, Jonesy. You're persistent."

"I don't intend to give up, ma'am."

She patted his arm. "I hope you never do."

Her comment raised his hopes. "May I see her?"

"I'm afraid she still refuses." She turned a pleasant smile to Lily. "She will, however, see you."

Lily gave him a look of sympathy. "I'll try to talk to her," she whispered as she moved around him and hurried through the door.

"You know where her room is, Lily," Mrs. Riley said. "Just go on back there."

"Thank you, ma'am."

Jonesy fought the envy rising inside him as he watched Lily disappear from view, while he wasn't even allowed past the front porch.

"Come on in, Jonesy. My daughter might not want to see you, but that doesn't mean I can't enjoy your company while you wait for Lily to come out."

"Thank you, ma'am." Jonesy stepped inside. "I appreciate the offer."

nine

Absolutely not. She would not see Jonesy no matter how many people he sent to speak for him.

"He's not going to stop," Lily said matter-of-factly.

"He will. Eventually."

Lily shook her head. "Trust me. I've never seen a man so determined. Why won't you see him? It's becoming ridiculous. Poor Jonesy. At least tell him to his face that you have no intention of marrying him."

"If I do, do you think he'll go away and leave me in peace?"

"If he truly believes that you aren't going to marry him, I think he'll give up. But he won't until he hears it from you."

Eva's legs trembled under the covers. "What if I write him a letter and you could give it to him?"

Lily's face screwed up into a scowl. "Don't be a coward."

"Coward? You think fear is what's keeping me from Jonesy?"

Lily's nod infuriated Eva. She was afraid of a lot of things nowadays, but telling Jonesy to go to Texas without her wasn't one of them. "All right. I'll see him." As soon as she said the words, she regretted them. "Wait."

But a smiling Lily was already across the room and had the door open.

Eva's mind whirled. Why had she given in to Lily's baiting so easily?

The sight of Jonesy filling the doorway made her stomach jump. "I must look awful."

A smile touched his lips, and he moved forward. "You're a sight for sore eyes."

False laughter gurgled in her throat. She dropped her gaze before his look of pity. "Always a romantic—even when you're telling a lie."

"I would never lie to you."

Silence pervaded the room, and suddenly Eva sensed his presence too deeply. She clutched the covers up to her throat.

Jonesy's eyes flickered over her. "It's so good to see you, Eva. How are you doing?"

The last thing she wanted to discuss with Jonesy was her ordeal. "I'm fine."

"Are you in a lot of pain?"

The truth was that only twinges and light bruising remained. But Eva was ashamed to admit it to him and try to explain why she was still in bed, unable to leave her room.

"Not a *lot* of pain anymore."

Admiration flickered in his eyes, making Eva feel even worse.

"Really, Jonesy, I'm almost all healed."

"How long before you can get a wedding planned?" The intensity of his gaze thrilled her and terrified her at the same time.

"Jonesy, please try to understand. I'm just not ready to leave my family."

"Then I'll wait."

"That's not going to do any good. I don't ever want to move to Texas." Eva fingered the flowers on her comforter.

"I'd like for you to go away and stop asking me. I'm not going to change my mind. Ever."

"Yes, you are." He said it with such finality that Eva almost said yes right then and there. But her common sense prevailed. "There are reasons." Her face burned, and she knew she must be flushed.

Jonesy remained silent for a long moment, until Eva ventured a glance into his face. His eyes were closed. "Jonesy?"

He opened his eyes and regarded her with sadness. "I don't know how to say this delicately. But I don't hold you responsible for what that man did to you." Stepping forward, he knelt beside the bed. Tears glistened in his eyes. "My love for you reaches so far beyond the physical that nothing matters except sharing my life with you."

The raw honesty shining from his eyes sifted all embarrassment from the conversation. Eva gave him the candid answer she had held in her heart for the past weeks. "I don't know if I could ever be a proper wife to you. I could cook and clean. I could keep you company and read poetry with you, but I don't know that I could ever sleep in your bed and bear your children."

The blood drained from his face as though he hadn't even considered that she might not want to share his bed. As though he'd only been thinking of his own reaction to the fact that she'd be coming to him tainted, unclean, impure, used goods.

Anger boiled inside her at his vanity. "I see that does matter to you. You don't mind that I've been used by another man as long as I let you use me, too." She turned away. "Get out, Jonesy. Go to Texas. Build your ranch and find a woman who wants to be your wife. Once and for all, will you please leave me in peace?"

Bitter pain twisted like a knife inside Eva's heart as Jonesy stood and left the room. She tightened her jaw and refused to give in to the sobs threatening just below the surface of her restraint. Tears would do no good.

Lily appeared a second later. "What happened? Jonesy looks positively ill."

Eva gave a short laugh. "I told him the truth. That I won't share his bed. I think that convinced him I'm not the woman for him."

A gasp escaped Lily's throat. "I don't know what to say."

Lily's face turned three shades of pink. Eva shook her head. What did delicacies matter anyway? Did they prepare a girl for the truth about relations between a man and a woman? Humiliation, fear, pain. She'd never give a man that kind of power over her again.

"Jonesy would never hurt you." Lily's voice had a troubled hesitance. As though she was trying to convince herself.

"Oh, Lily. You know nothing about it."

"Billy wants me to marry him." She said the statement flatly. Eva grimaced. A month ago, they would have squealed and giggled and started to make plans for the big day.

Instead Eva shrugged, her numbed emotions unable to muster even cursory excitement for her childhood friend. "I hope you'll be very happy. I know Billy has always cared for you."

"Y–you don't think I should say yes?"

Eva looked at her evenly. "I would never encourage any woman to put herself through the things a woman must endure to be a wife to any man. Even a good one."

Lily's voice trembled, but Eva felt no remorse. She'd

simply told the truth. What sort of friend would she be if she allowed Lily to enter into marriage with the same naive beliefs with which every other woman entered the institution?

A soft tap on the door preceded Ma's entrance. "Lily, Jonesy said he needs to take you home so he can help his pa with chores."

"Yes, ma'am."

Ma looked from Eva to Lily. Her brow wrinkled. "What's wrong?"

"Nothing, Mrs. Riley." Lily turned to Eva. "Good-bye, Eva. I'll come see you again soon." But as she left, Eva had the sinking sensation that she wouldn't be back.

Hope turned her questioning gaze to Eva. "Did you two have a disagreement?"

"No."

"Then why is Lily as white as a sheet and about to cry?"

"Well, if you must know, Lily told me Billy asked her to marry him."

Joy spread a wide smile across Ma's face. "It's about time that brother of yours got around to marrying that girl. I was afraid she'd find someone else. You don't look a bit happy. Isn't this what you've always hoped for? Lily and you will truly be sisters now."

Eva shrugged. "We're not children anymore. Besides, I know about what happens in a marriage. And now Lily does, too."

Ma's eyes widened in horror. "What did you tell her?"

"The truth."

"Oh, Eva. It's not that way between a husband and wife who love each other. What happened to you was a violent act of evil. Love is gentle and kind and patient."

"Ma, please. I'd rather not discuss this."

Ma moved to the door, a heavy sigh pushing from her lungs. "All right. I'll leave you alone. But I'm having your pa fix a tub for you later."

"No! I don't want to."

"Eva Star Riley. The whole house is beginning to smell bad. You are going to take a bath, and I'm going to wash your bedding. And that's final. Furthermore, you will take your meals with the rest of us from now on. And, honey, no more slop jar. You'll have to begin walking to the outhouse again."

"How can you treat me this way after what I've been through?" Tears of fury burned her eyes. "I cannot endure more mistreatment."

"Eva Riley, you're my darling daughter, and my heart aches for what you've been through. If I could take away the memories and the pain and fear, I would. But I can't. We have all tried to help you through the healing. But you must start living again, darling. You can't stay hidden away in your bedroom for the rest of your life."

She left the room, closing the door firmly behind her. Eva pounded the bed with her fists. Why couldn't she stay tucked away, safe in her little cocoon? The thought of venturing beyond her bedroom door filled her with trepidation.

Panic rose. In an instant, she threw the covers over her head and lay shaking beneath the heavy quilts.

❧

Jonesy found himself at a crossroads. If he turned right, the road would lead the wagon home, where his pa waited for him to help with the evening chores. Left would take him back to the Rileys' home, where Eva would either agree to see him or once more jab a knife into his already bleeding heart.

Everything in him wanted to take the road to the left. To plead with her to reconsider, to give him a chance to prove his love for her.

Lily had been silent and shaken on the way back to town. But try as he might, Jonesy couldn't convince her to open up about what Eva had told her that upset her so. Finally he'd given up and allowed her the solitude she seemed to need. Maybe that's all Eva needed, as well. Perhaps if he gave her a little more time, she'd change her mind. It was too late for him to begin the four-and-a-half-month journey back to Texas now; he'd have to wait until after the winter.

If Eva needed time, he had it to give her. He turned the wagon to the right.

❧

"Please, Pa," Eva moaned. "Please don't make me."

Pa's eyes clouded with indecision, but he remained as resolute as Ma. "I'm sorry, Papoose. But your ma's right. I'll hold your hand until we get to the kitchen. Then your ma will stay with you while you take your bath. Trust me. You're going to feel much better after you're clean."

Eva stopped fighting. If Pa wasn't on her side, then there was no hope. Her body shook with fear, and she clung to Pa as they walked slowly to the door. A step past the threshold, her knees buckled as fear gripped her throat. "Pa."

"Shh, I'm here." He swept her up in his arms and carried her the rest of the way to the kitchen.

"She'll be all right," Ma's quiet voice assured as Pa set her on her feet on the kitchen floor. He nodded, pressed a kiss to Eva's head, and walked back through the kitchen to the living room and went outside.

Eva glanced at the tub of water, and relief moved through her. Now that she'd left her room, a weight seemed lifted from her shoulders.

Ma helped her undress and get into the tub. Eva closed her eyes and sank down into the warm water. "I'll be okay, Ma. I know you want to get my bedding."

A smile spread across Ma's face. "You sure?"

Eva regarded her mother. Circles darkened the skin beneath her eyes, and her dress hung on her as though she'd lost weight. "Are you all right, Ma?"

"I think I will be now, darling. If you're all right, I will be."

Eva reached out a wet hand and took her ma's. "Thank you for forcing me to do this. I never would have left that room on my own."

When she was alone, Eva closed her eyes once more and allowed the warm water to loosen the dirt caked onto her skin.

ten

Lady Anne cantered as though she were aware that today was the Lord's Day and she had the distinct honor of carrying Jonesy to the worship service.

A blast of colder-than-usual air whipped up, forcing Jonesy to turn up his collar. He shivered against the wind and glanced at the cloudy sky. It seemed as though Hobbs and the surrounding area might be in for a hard winter. Good thing he'd decided against trying to make it to Texas before spring. He might have gotten stuck in Wyoming.

It had been almost a week since he'd seen Eva, and he still couldn't quite bring himself to believe what she had indicated. She could cook and clean but not share his bed? Hurt burned through him like a branding iron. Did she honestly believe he would harm her the way Pete had? Did she think it would be the same?

The thought that she could even consider such a thing filled him with shame. How did a single man explain to the woman he loved that he wanted to hold her in his arms until dawn? Bring her silky curls to his face and lose himself in the sweet scent of lilac that always seemed to cling to her? There weren't words to explain those things to a young, unmarried woman. Tenderness, adoration, and love were things a young husband had to wait until the night of his wedding to express.

Father, I don't want to lose Eva. How do I convince her that I mean her only good? That I would never harm her?

The answer didn't come in the wind.

As he entered the churchyard, his heart leaped. Eva's pa was helping her from the wagon. Jonesy's throat tightened at the sight of her, frail and pale. She looked as though she might bolt at a loud noise or a sudden movement. She seemed positively terrified.

It took only a moment to tie Lady Anne to a post and meet the Rileys at the door. Eva's eyes were guarded, and she gave him only a cursory smile when he greeted her.

"Nice to see you here, Eva."

"Thank you." She nodded as though to dismiss him.

Mr. Riley clapped him on the shoulder. "We'll talk to you after the service, Jonesy."

"Yes, sir."

Jonesy fought the urge to stare at Eva all through the service. He wasn't sure how many people knew what had happened to her. Certainly her family and friends wouldn't have made it known. But one never knew what the town gossips were whispering about.

Pastor Greg opened the service with the answer to the question Jonesy had asked of the Lord. "Charity suffers long and is kind."

After the reading of 1 Corinthians 13:5, everything else Greg said was tuned out of Jonesy's mind. He zeroed in on that single, short verse that stated charity "seeketh not her own."

Are you trying to tell me I'm selfish? he asked the Lord.

Selfish? Him? Hadn't he left his land to come help his pa? Hadn't he been willing to put his own plans on hold for almost two years in order to honor his father and mother?

Selfish? Surely he was hearing the Lord wrong. He'd even been willing to wait until spring so Eva could have a proper wedding. . .before everything happened.

Deep in thought, he would have missed the closing prayer if his ma hadn't nudged him. He stood as they sang the doxology.

The crowded little sanctuary left little room to move quickly. With the Rileys sitting close to the back of the building and his family near the front, by the time Jonesy exited the church, the Rileys' wagon had disappeared. He knew he could easily catch up with them, but he wanted to speak to Eva in private.

"Don't worry, son."

Jonesy turned at the sound of his mother's voice.

"You'll see her tonight. Eva and her parents are coming for supper."

A grin spread across his face.

She slipped her hand through the crook in his arm, and he escorted her down the church steps and to the wagon.

"How do you think she looked, Ma?"

His mother gave him a troubled frown. "Eva seems very frail, doesn't she?"

He nodded. "I can't bear it."

"She's getting better, though. Today was the first time she's been in church in six weeks. Be patient with her, Ben. Eva loves you. She just has to get past the fear."

"I know, Ma. I'm trying. I keep praying that she'll learn to trust me again."

Ma placed a hand on his shoulder. "Maybe it's time to start praying that she'll learn to trust God again. Seems to me all your praying is for your sake, not Eva's."

Jonesy considered her words the rest of the day. Ma was right. So was the Lord. He had been acting selfishly. It was time for him to stop thinking of how her ordeal affected his life and start thinking of how he could help her heal.

❧

During supper, conversation remained lighthearted. Mrs. Riley and Ma discussed the upcoming Christmas dance, while Pa and Mr. Riley talked about the rising price of grain and the rancher who had recently bought land just a few miles to the north. Despite Pa's experience as a rancher, he was a farmer now and worried that ranchers would come in and take up all the farmland with their cattle and horses.

Eva sat pale and still, taking only a few bites of her food in an effort, Jonesy suspected, to be polite. It was obvious her heart wasn't in the meal, though she kept her eyes downcast.

Jonesy kept his own gaze fixed on her, hoping she would look up and catch his eye. She had come such a long way from the dirty, unkempt, angry woman of a week ago. But he could see she had a long way to go.

"Ben, why don't you take Eva out to the barn and show her the new puppies?"

Eva jerked her head up at the sound of Jonesy's ma's voice. Interest flashed in her fawnlike eyes.

Jonesy winked at her. "Lord Byron's a pa. Want to see his young'uns?"

A smile tipped the corners of her mouth. "I'd love to."

Her eagerness sent a sense of relief through Jonesy. His chair scraped the floor as he pushed back from the table.

Eva stood, as well. "Dinner was delicious, Mrs. Jones. Thank you."

"You're welcome."

Eva followed Jonesy outside.

"Trust Ma to ease a tense situation."

"What do you mean?"

"I think she could tell you weren't exactly enjoying the company."

Horror widened Eva's eyes. "Oh my. I didn't mean to be rude. I'd better go back inside and apologize."

Jonesy caught her arm.

"Eva, it's all right. She isn't offended. That's why she offered you a way out of there. To tell you the truth, I was wondering how long I was going to have to sit there and make polite conversation so as not to be rude to your parents. Ma took pity on us both."

Eva gave a soft laugh. Not the throaty, rich laugh that used to come from the depths of her belly. But the sound still sent chills down Jonesy's spine.

Lord Byron gave an excited bark and nearly knocked Eva down when they walked into the barn.

Jonesy laughed. "Seems as though someone's missed you."

Eva ruffled Lord Byron's fur. "So you've gone and found yourself a wife, you crazy mutt."

"Mutt?" Jonesy said with mock offense. "Lord Byron is nobility. Keep a respectful tone in your voice, or we'll be forced to banish you to the tower."

"I'm sorry, old boy."

Lord Byron pranced to the back of the barn, then came halfway back and stood expectantly. Jonesy nudged Eva. "Look. He wants to show off his puppies."

"Well, that is what we're here for. Let's not disappoint him."

The wiggling half-dozen puppies were a mix from a

pitch-black mother dog and Lord Byron, whose white, brown, and black patches had no rhyme or reason.

"Ah, so this must be the missus." Eva knelt beside the nursing litter. "And what is her name?" She smiled. "I know she isn't Lady Anne. That name's taken."

"Her name is Beauty."

"Beauty?"

" 'She walks in beauty, like the night.' From the poetry of Lord Byron."

"Ah. Appropriate." She grinned.

One brown-and-white puppy detached itself from its mother and moved blindly on weak, wobbly newborn legs.

A breath of compassion left Eva's throat. "The sweet little thing." She reached down and took the fat, wiggling pup between her palms and cuddled it close. Jonesy held his breath as she rubbed her cheek against the soft fur.

On impulse, he reached forward to brush a curl from Eva's cheek. She gasped and jerked back, her eyes alight with fear. "What are you doing?" she croaked out.

"You had some hair in your face. I was. . .I'm sorry."

She set the puppy down gently next to its mother and watched while it nudged its way in among its warm, furry brothers and sisters. Standing, Eva gathered a shaky breath. "I'd like to go back inside now. I should help our mothers clean up."

"Eva, I'm sorry."

"It's all right, Jonesy." But he could see she was far from all right.

"Just a couple more minutes? I'd like to talk to you about something."

"Please, Jonesy. I said all I have to say about marrying

you. Don't make this any harder."

Charity suffereth long and is kind. It seeketh not her own.

"Here's the thing." Jonesy summoned the courage to say what he had to say. "I know things have changed. I wish I were the sort of man who could honestly tell you that I could still marry you and never think about taking you into my bed. But that's just not true. As much as I love you, I'm still a man."

"I don't see why we have to have this discussion again."

The sound of Eva's anger spurred him on to explain before she completely cut him off and went inside without hearing him out. "I love you, Eva. And I still want to marry you. But I don't want to lose my friendship with you. I've shared my dreams with you, my poetry, my hope for the future. I miss our rides together and our talks by the river. So if you'll consider it, I'd like us to be friends again. As a matter of fact, I take back my proposal. Consider yourself unasked to be my wife."

An uncertain smile tipped her lips. "You're a little crazy, you know that?"

"Yeah, I know."

"I miss our talks, too, Jonesy. And our rides."

"Does that mean you're willing to take me back into your life as a friend?"

"I guess that's all we were meant to be." She looked up at him, daring him to refute it.

"Maybe so." But he didn't believe that for a second.

"Does this mean you're staying in Oregon until spring?"

Jonesy nodded. "I can't take a chance on getting stuck somewhere because of the weather. I'd rather wait it out here."

"I'm glad."

❧

Eva rode Patches carefully. The horse still seemed to be favoring his left hind leg where the bullet had gone in. Pa's assurance that he needed to work it in order to gain strength was the only thing that could convince Eva to put a saddle on his back and ride him. "He needs to get his confidence back up," Pa had said. "Nothing worse for a horse than to feel helpless."

The early December wind brought with it an icy chill that predicted a cold, harsh winter. Eva shivered and pulled her pa's sheepskin coat closer about her. She cast a sideways glance at Jonesy. They were almost to the river, and neither had spoken more than five words. But it was enough that they be together. Enough that he wanted to be her friend, even if nothing in the relationship went deeper.

"All the geese are gone," she said. "Last time I was here, they hadn't yet flown south for the winter."

"They'll be back."

Eva dismounted and dropped Patches's reins. The horse moved to the river and dipped his head for a drink. "It's still sad to see them go. I know it's silly, but I like to watch them fly away. I always bring bread to feed them. It's sort of my way of telling them good-bye and wishing them Godspeed on their journey."

"I think that's sweet."

"You do, huh?" Eva felt a familiar frustration. Even more unnerving was the fact that she didn't understand where the frustration came from. The old Jonesy would have tugged her long braid and called her a sentimental fool. But this Jonesy was careful. Tender, watchful. Like a man in love, not a friend. It kept her on her guard with him. She longed for their easy camaraderie to return.

Jonesy gave a short laugh as though reading her thoughts. "All right, maybe it's a little eccentric to have a going-away party for a flock of geese."

"Well, it's no more crazy than naming your dog after a poet."

That wonderful, boyish grin spread across his mouth. Eva felt herself relax as she looked out over the water. Jonesy looped Lady Anne's reins around a nearby bush. He walked to their tree and slid down the trunk. "Come sit with me, Eva."

"It's a little cold to be sitting on the ground, don't you think?"

"Cold? This is nothing."

Eva smiled when he shivered and wrapped his arms around himself. Her heart nearly stopped when he opened his arms and legs.

"Come sit against me, and we'll keep each other warm."

Anxiety began to build. "Jonesy. . ."

"All right then. I'll scoot over, and you can sit next to me." He did so and patted the ground. "It's all right. I'll keep my hands to myself."

Eva sat next to him. They stared silently across the water. Eva leaned her head back, enjoying her time with Jonesy. The solid strength of his shoulder pressing against hers surprised her. And the fact that she didn't cringe at his touch.

They sat in silence. There was no need to fill the space between them with empty chatter. The only thing that mattered was being in the open together. Watching the river and listening to the birds in the trees.

Eva closed her eyes. She didn't know how long they remained there, but eventually, despite the cold, her tension faded and peace covered her.

Finally Jonesy's voice broke the silence. " 'He leadeth me beside the still waters. He restoreth my soul.' "

"Do you think that's really possible?" Her voice sounded small, like a child's, but Eva had mustered all of her strength just to gain that much volume.

"What? Having your soul restored?"

Eva nodded but didn't open her eyes. "I don't see how I'll ever be the same person I was before."

"Experiences change us, honey. Some are good experiences, some bad. It's all right to be a little rattled at first, but ultimately it's up to us how we change forever."

Eva gave a short laugh and looked at him. "At least when something good happens, you know the change will be good. How can good come from something bad?"

"I've known fellows who find gold and get rich quick, and believe me, some don't change for the better. It's what's in a person's heart that determines how life's tests and trials will change him or her. The Bible says when believers are tried by fire, we come out pure gold. It's up to us to decide whether to take the tests and become purified or resist the testing and become bitter."

Eva stared, slack-jawed. "You mean to tell me that you think God is testing me by letting this thing happen? How can something like this make me a better person?"

"No," he said. "God doesn't do evil to people to test them. At least I don't believe so. But in the aftermath of that evil, we have some tough choices to make. Do we trust

God? Do we allow His still waters to restore us? Or will we fight and kick and wallow in the mire of self-pity until we destroy ourselves?"

Anger flashed through Eva, and she shot to her feet. "That's what you think of me, is it? You think I am choosing to be angry and bitter and wallow in the mud like a pig? All this because I won't marry you and allow you to maul me for the rest of my life?"

Jonesy shoved up beside her, his eyes reflecting her anger and frustration. "You're twisting my words. You know that's not what I meant. And maul you? Do you honestly think I'd hurt one inch of your body? I love you." He reached out to touch her arm.

Instant fear surged inside Eva. A scream started in her belly and shot from her lips.

"Eva, honey. I'm sorry."

But Eva wouldn't hear him. All she could do was scream.

His arms encircled her, and he held her tightly. "It's all right, Eva. No one is going to hurt you. Do you understand? I love you. I love you. I love you."

In the recesses of her mind, the words began to penetrate. Her screams turned to sobs, and her fighting turned to clinging. Jonesy's arms were no longer to be feared, but arms to run to. She clutched at him. "Hold me, Jonesy. Don't let me go. Please don't go."

In a beat, Eva's stomach rebelled. She pulled away just in time to avoid retching all over him. When she was finished, he handed her a handkerchief.

"I'm sorry, Jonesy. I don't know what came over me."

"You can't help getting sick."

"I mean fighting you and screaming."

He stroked her head, and Eva allowed the soft touch. Welcomed it, in fact. "You couldn't help that either. Now let's get you home so your ma can put you to bed."

eleven

Jonesy stared in horrified disbelief as his mother relayed the news. "How could that be?"

"Son, Eva's been sick every day since shortly after that awful day. Hope finally sent Andy for Doc Smith. There's no question that she's with child."

"And Eva asked her ma to tell us instead of telling me herself?"

Ma nodded grimly. "She can't face you. It was hard enough just having the man she loves know what had happened to her. But this. . .it's too much for any woman to endure."

Just when he was starting to get through to her. Just when she was opening up, allowing his arms to hold her. Now she wouldn't see him again? "When will her suffering end? When?" He leaned forward, elbows on his knees, and buried his face in his hands.

Ma stood behind him, rubbing his back. He heard her softly praying for peace.

"I've been praying that God would allow her to forget so she can heal on the inside and start to live again. Now she's going to have a baby as a reminder for the rest of her life." He took to his feet as a thought entered his mind. "She has to marry me now."

"Son, Eva needs some time to adjust to this. I pray she'll come around again, just like she did before. But now's not the time to press her."

"Don't you see, though? The baby changes things. She needs a husband so people won't gossip."

"People can count the months, son. They'll assume you and Eva fell into sin and had to get married. Either way, Eva will have to bear the burden of public scrutiny. But if you marry her suddenlike, you'll have to bear it, too."

"Not if I move her away after the baby's born. No one in Texas will know anything about Eva or what happened to her. They'll assume we married here and waited until the baby was born and old enough to move. There's no reason for anyone to question whether or not the baby's mine. Eva's reputation wouldn't be in jeopardy."

Jonesy kissed his mother's cheek. "Don't wait supper for me."

His mind churned with the possibilities all the way to the Rileys' home. Eva thought she didn't want to be a wife to him. But once she held that baby in her arms, she'd want another one. And then she'd turn to him. *God, was this Your plan all along?*

Charity suffereth long and is kind. It seeketh not her own.

I am being long-suffering and kind and selfless. I'm taking a woman who is with child by another man and making her my wife!

Eva would know, now, how much he loved her.

Ten minutes later, he stood on the Rileys' porch, looking into the sympathetic eyes of Mrs. Riley.

"I'm sorry, Jonesy. Eva's gone to stay with her cousin Aimee in Oregon City. She won't be home for quite some time."

"But I want to marry her. I'll be a pa to her baby, Mrs.

Riley. We can go to Texas, where no one knows."

"Eva will always know." Tears flooded her eyes. "I've never seen her this way. Even after she was attacked, she still had fight in her. Now it's as though all the life has flowed from her veins. I'm afraid for her, Jonesy."

"I have to see her."

Hope touched her fingers to his forearm. "If you love her, you'll let her go. She can't face you right now. Her shame cuts so deeply that seeing you and knowing she can't be yours, pure and untouched, is more than she'll be able to bear. I fear what it might do to her."

All the strength left his legs, and he sank to a wooden rocking chair on the porch. He stared silently into the chilled air.

"I'm sorry, Jonesy. This is for the best. Eva wants to be left alone. I think you need to respect her wishes this time."

Nodding, he rose slowly. "Yes, ma'am." He walked down the steps and mounted Lady Anne. "If you write her a letter, will you please tell her I love her and that I'm praying for her every day?"

"I will, Jonesy. I will."

❧

Eva followed her cousin down a long hallway in the spacious Donnelly home. "This is lovely, Aimes," she said. "Who'd have ever thought when you adopted Georgie that you'd end up living in a mansion with the boy's pa?"

"It's not quite a mansion." Aimee chuckled. "But I couldn't be happier married to Rex and raising Georgie." She stopped before a closed door and turned the handle. With a smile, she pushed the door open. "What do you think?"

Eva drew a breath. A four-poster bed sat against the far wall, covered by a lovely white comforter with lace around the edges. The windows were framed by lacy white curtains that matched the comforter. A lovely maple-wood wardrobe presided over the room and towered above Eva.

"It's extra tall because there's a storage shelf on top," Aimee explained.

"Oh."

Aimee nodded to the carriage driver who had carried Eva's bags up the stairs. "Thank you, Mr. Marlow."

"You're welcome, ma'am. If you need anything else, please ring for me." He bowed out of the room.

Aimee walked to the bed and sat. "Come sit down, and let's talk for a moment."

Fatigued beyond anything she'd ever felt, Eva untied her black bonnet and sank onto the feather mattress.

"You must be exhausted," Aimee said. "Lie back, and I'll take your boots off for you."

Heat warmed Eva's cheeks. "That's not necessary. Really."

"Nonsense. You are here to be taken care of. So let me do that for you."

Eva gave a bitter snort. "I'm not here to be taken care of—just to get out of the way while I have this baby. I think Ma and Pa can't bear to see me. My presence reminds them of what happened to me."

Aimee loosened both boots and set them on the floor. "Eva, do you know why I chose this room for you?"

Eva shook her head.

"I call this the angels' room because it's so beautiful and white. As though the angels needed a place of purity and perfection, so they made this room for themselves."

"Then I shouldn't be here."

"Yes, you should. The white is to remind you that in the eyes of God you are as pure as the day you were born. You are His child, washed in the blood of the Lamb and made pure by His suffering. Now I want you to lie in this bed every night and say this aloud to yourself: 'I am not responsible for what happened to me. It was not my sin that caused this innocent child to exist. I am not to blame.' " Aimee looked at her firmly. "Can you do that?"

"I'll try, Aimes; I promise I'll try." But Eva knew she couldn't. Aimee was sweet and meant well, but some things were just impossible to make someone else understand.

"My ma once told me a very personal story about her past that few other people know. I asked her if I could share it with you, and she gave me permission. Would you like to hear it?"

Curiosity piqued, Eva nodded. "Of course."

"You know I was just a little girl, maybe four or five, when my pa married my ma, right?"

"Yes."

"Well, not many people know that her ma was a saloon girl."

A gasp escaped Eva's throat. "You mean she was a . . ."

"Prostitute, yes." A blush spread across Aimee's already rosy cheeks. "My ma was raised above a saloon, knowing what her ma did to make a living."

Now it was Eva's turn to blush.

"When her ma was killed by the owner of Luke's Saloon, she had to run away or risk being forced into the same life."

Eva kept her eyes on Aimee, riveted by this part of her aunt's life she'd known nothing about.

"Even though her ma was a saloon girl, she was loving and kind. But she had to fight to keep my ma. Luke had demanded she get rid of her."

"You mean put her in an orphanage?"

"Yes. He even threatened to do it himself. But even before she was born, Luke wanted my ma's ma to go to a woman he knew who helped women get rid of babies they didn't want."

Eva's eyes grew wide. She'd never heard of such a thing. "Do you mean there's a way to get rid of a baby before it's born?"

Aimee gave her a sharp look. "It's murder. And even a prostitute who didn't know the Lord knew better than to do such a thing. Don't forget, Eva. The Bible says that God knew us even before we were formed in our mothers' wombs. He knows that child you're carrying. He knows who he or she was created to be. There are no accidents in God's kingdom. He has a purpose for your baby's life."

Once more heat spread across Eva's face. "I'm sure you're right," she mumbled.

"Anyway," Aimee said, "my ma met my pa while she was running away, and he saved her and brought her to Grammy."

"I love the story of how they fell in love."

"What you don't know is that my ma was ashamed to tell Pa about her past. Where she came from. She was afraid he wouldn't understand that she was the daughter of a prostitute."

"But that wasn't her fault."

"You're right. And, Eva, you have to understand that none of this is your fault either. God's grace is more than sufficient to get you through this birth. This baby is as innocent as you are, and Jesus already loves your little one, no matter how he or she was brought into this world. God is forming the little fingers and toes. The mouth that will someday smile at you and melt your heart."

Eva listened halfheartedly to Aimee's speech. She felt no affection for this child whom Jesus apparently already knew. The only thing she could think of was how to find a woman who might help her.

❧

Eva shivered in the dark. From fear, from cold, from the guilt of what she was going to do if everything went according to plan.

She fought back nausea and fear as she walked for an hour to reach the seedier side of town, where the saloons and gambling halls were located. It had taken her a few days to gather the courage to ask one of the maids in the house about it. Reluctantly, and only after payment of a string of pearls Eva's pa had given her for her birthday when she turned sixteen, had the young woman given her directions.

Following the sound of loud, high-pitched laughter, she walked into the first saloon at the end of the street. The raucous laughter receded until finally the room was quiet.

Eva thought she might faint from fear. What had she been thinking? Men who went to bars were not good, God-fearing people. They might be like. . .but she couldn't think about that now. If she did, she wouldn't have the courage to do what she needed to do.

As she walked by a table of men, she felt herself being tugged downward. She let out a scream, and before she quite knew what was happening, she landed in the lap of a laughing, intoxicated man. "Hey, honey, you're a little overdressed to be one of Mike's girls, ain't ya?"

Eva struggled to her feet, shaking in fear. "I'm not one of M–Mike's girls. Now leave me be."

The men let up a roar of laughter.

"What do you want, lady?" the man behind the bar called. "If you ain't lookin' for a job, how 'bout you get on outta here? These men don't want to be reminded of their wives."

"If I had me a wife what looked like her, I would," called a slurred voice. "My wife's fat and bossy."

Eva tried to ignore the suggestive calls and comments. She leveled her gaze at the man behind the counter and lowered her voice. "I need to speak with one of the young women who work here."

"Which one?"

"I–it doesn't matter, I guess. Someone who has worked here for a while."

"Now look here, sister." He poked at her face with a grimy finger. "You leave the preachin' to Sundays. My girls ain't interested in gettin' baptized."

"I assure you, I'm not here to proselytize. I need some information."

Eva had never felt so dirty in her life. She had to close her mind off to what she was about to do, or she couldn't endure it.

"I don't know what you want," the bartender said, "but I'll give you a few minutes. Sally! Get over here."

Eva turned as a young woman with red hair and heavy cosmetics sashayed across the room. Eva's cheeks burned at the sight of her scantily clad figure.

"Whatcha need, Mike?"

"This girl wants to talk to one of the girls."

Sally's eyes went cold as she gave Eva the once-over. "Well, I don't want to talk to the likes of her." She started to turn, but Mike snatched her wrist. She gasped and grimaced.

"I say you're gonna talk to her. And you're gonna do as you're told."

"All right, Mike. I'll talk to her. Don't break my arm, or I won't be able to work."

He scowled and let her go. "You just mind how you're talkin' to me from now on if you know what's good for ya."

"Sure, Mike. Sorry." She turned her icy glare back to Eva. "What's a respectable lady like you doing in a place like Mike's? You crazy or something? Or are you looking for your husband? 'Cause if he came in here, I probably know him." She looked at Eva with smug insolence, daring her to fight back.

Her hostility surprised Eva. She had seen people walk across the street to avoid sharing a sidewalk with a saloon girl, but it had never occurred to her that the feeling might be mutual coming from the other side of the street.

"I don't have a husband, and I couldn't care less how many men you know." She gave Sally a smug look in return. "I need some information. But if you don't want to give it to me, I'll go elsewhere."

The woman's brow furrowed. "What do you mean?"

"I really don't want to discuss it here. Can we go somewhere private?" Fortunately, the men seemed to have lost interest, and the calls and comments had mostly stopped.

Still, Eva didn't want to take a chance that someone might be listening.

"Mike, we'll be in your office," Sally said across the bar.

"Hurry up," he growled. "I ain't losin' money tonight so you can go have girly talk."

Sally led her to a rough little room containing a settee and a rough-hewn wooden desk with a chair. Eva sank against the closed door and regarded Sally evenly. Her heart raced.

The other young woman leaned against the desk and shrugged. "So what can you possibly want to know so badly that you'd traipse all the way over to this side of town? And don't say you're not from the rich part of town, because I can tell from your clothes and your manners."

Eva sniffed and raised her chin. "Actually, I don't even live in Oregon City. I'm staying with my cousin and her husband for a while."

Eva felt the woman's scrutiny. She would receive no sympathy from someone who had probably been used by more men than she could count. Eva knew if she had a prayer of obtaining help, she would have to be civil. "I need to know how I can find someone who will help me with a problem."

"What kind of problem?"

"I'm with child."

Amusement crinkled in the woman's blue eyes. "I see. And the baby's father doesn't want to marry you? Let me guess. He's already married. Or maybe you can't let your rich daddy know you fell in love with the ranch hand who isn't nearly good enough for you." She chuckled. "Honey, you're no better than I am, are you?"

Shaking in anger, Eva stomped across the room and slapped the girl's face. "How dare you laugh at me! I'm not like you at all. I didn't give myself to a man. I was accosted. I hate the man who did this to me. And I hate this baby. I want it out of me. And I figure a woman like you must know how to do that."

Sally rubbed her cheek where Eva had struck her. "I don't like to be hit." She strode to the door. "I'm leaving."

Eva clutched her arm. "Please help me! I'm sorry I slapped you. You have every right to be angry with me. But you have to understand. I had no choice in this. I have already lost everything I love as a result of this, and now I'm going to have this monster's baby? How much more must I endure?" Eva sank to the floor and buried her face in her hands.

Sally knelt in front of her. "All right. I'm sorry I laughed at you. But are you sure you want to do this? Don't you have family who will take care of you and a baby?"

"Can you help me or not?"

Sally gave a reluctant nod. "I know someone. But I have to warn you. She's mean. And she'll probably try to force you to stay and work for her."

"But I don't need a job."

Sally gave a short laugh. "Honey, you really are green, aren't you?"

"I don't know what you mean."

"Never mind. You think long and hard about doing this. It's dangerous. A lot of women die from it."

Eva shuddered at the thought of dying in such a manner. She wrapped her arms around herself. "I would rather be dead than have to raise this baby."

"All right. It's your choice. But you'll have to wait until I finish for the night. Stay in here and keep the door locked. Those men aren't even wound up yet." She pointed to the settee, which had a blanket hanging over its side. "Lie down and try to sleep. I'll come get you in the morning."

"In the morning? Why can't we go tonight?"

She gave a short laugh and walked toward the door, her pink satin gown swishing against black stockings. "Honey, I don't get off work until dawn, when the men run out of money and go home to their families."

twelve

Jonesy woke with a start, his heart racing wildly in his chest. Something was wrong. He'd dreamed of Eva, and she was crying and reaching out to him. His body shook as he relived the dream. Her hands dripped with blood. Her lips didn't move, but he could hear the cry of her heart. *Help me. Help me, Jonesy.*

Unable to push aside the image, he shoved back the covers and swung his legs over the side of the bed. He'd never felt so helpless in all his life. Leaning forward, he began to pray.

"Father, keep Eva safe. Please show her Your love for her. Show her Your mercy."

He prayed for an hour. Then he stood and paced and prayed for another hour. When dawn began to break, he knew he had to make the trip to Oregon City. Even if Eva wouldn't see him, he had to see for himself that she was all right.

As silently as possible, he grabbed his saddlebag and stuffed a clean shirt into it, followed by his Bible and extra bullets for his gun, just in case he had need of it.

He carried his boots as he left his room and passed through the living room. He'd wait until he got to the porch to pull them on. He didn't want to wake up Ma and Pa.

Just as he pulled his Stetson off the hat rack, he got the scare of his life.

"Where you going, son?" His ma's voice came out of nowhere.

"You scared me half to death, Ma."

She sat in front of the fire, wearing her robe and a nightcap, rocking in her chair. Her long gray hair was braided and slung over both shoulders. "I asked you a question. Where do you think you're sneaking off to before dawn?"

"Sneaking off? Ma, I'm a grown man."

"Grown men don't sneak off in the middle of the night rather than have to face their parents."

"Oh, all right. I'm going to go to Oregon City and find Eva. I had a horrible dream last night about her, and I need to see her."

"I've been hearing you up there. I imagine you've been praying all night just like I have. But going to Oregon City isn't a good idea. Not until you're invited. God woke you up to pray. That's all. Now Eva and her parents have both asked you not to pressure Eva. I think you need to honor their request."

"You didn't see what I saw in that dream, Ma. The look in her eyes. She reached out to me."

"And there was blood on her hands?"

Stunned, Jonesy nodded.

"The Lord gave me the same dream, son. Why do you think I'm up at this hour? I've been praying all night, right alongside you. Now do you think God's telling us both to go to Oregon City?"

"No."

"That's right. He's not telling me to go, and you are not to go either. The only thing God is asking of us right now is to bombard heaven with prayers on behalf of that girl. And I'm sure her ma and pa are also praying for her at this moment."

"What does it mean, though? All the blood?"

"I don't know, but it's not good. That's why we have to keep praying until God gives us peace that Eva's all right again."

Jonesy dropped his boots, hung his Stetson back on the hat rack, and slid his saddlebag from his shoulder. "You win. Let's pray."

❧

Eva fought to catch her breath from the rapid pace Sally set. She also fought to contain her nausea as the young woman walked her through the fetid alleyway behind the saloon. "Could you please slow down just a little?" she asked.

"Look, if you want to do this, you'll have to hurry. Bea's been workin' all night, too. If we don't get there soon, she'll be sleeping, and you'll have to wait until later. Maybe even tomorrow."

Eva picked up the pace. "I'll try to keep up."

In a few moments, they reached the back door of what Eva could only surmise was a house of ill repute. It wasn't even disguised as a saloon. Sally knocked, and they waited until a large man answered the door.

"You don't work here anymore," he grumbled. "What do you want?"

"I'm here to see Bea."

The man ogled Eva. "You bringin' her another girl to replace you?"

"No. She ain't like that."

"Then what's she doing with you?"

"That's none of your business. Go tell Bea I need to talk to her."

"Wait here." The door closed, and Eva stood shivering in the cold, foul-smelling alley. Her stomach revolted, and she rushed to the other side of the alley.

When she was finished, Sally handed her a perfumed hanky. "Keep it. I got lots more."

"Thanks." Eva wiped her mouth, fighting nausea once more from the musky scent in the cloth.

The door opened, and the most beautiful woman Eva had ever seen stood there smiling. Eva couldn't take her eyes off her hair, which was just a little too blond to be real.

"Sally, darling. It's wonderful to see you again. Have you finally given up on Mike?"

"No," she said crisply. "And I never will."

The woman sighed and waved them inside. "Ah, well, I had hoped. Who is this?" She pointed at Eva.

"She's in a fix, Bea. I thought maybe you might could help her."

Anxiety began to build inside Eva. She shouldn't be here. How would she ever face her ma again, knowing she'd associated with these sorts of people?

"Honey, you'd better sit down. You look like you're about to pass out." Bea took her arm and escorted her to a kitchen chair. "Now tell Bea all about it."

"She was raped," Sally broke in flatly, without emotion, as though it didn't matter. "She wants to do away with the baby and forget it ever happened."

Do away with the baby? Suddenly Eva saw a fat, pink

baby with rosy lips and soft brown hair. Was it a boy or a girl?

No. She couldn't think about that. She'd go crazy if she did. Tears burned her eyes.

The woman placed an arm around Eva's shoulders and clicked her tongue sympathetically. "There, there, we'll have you fixed up in no time. A beauty like you shouldn't be saddled with a baby at this time in your life. Especially a baby conceived in such a wretched circumstance."

Eva's unease increased. She stood. "I—I think perhaps I've made a mistake. I should probably go."

"Well, it's certainly up to you. If you want to see that man's face the rest of your life, every time you look at his child."

Bea walked to the counter and pulled out a cup and saucer. She set the teakettle on to boil, leaving Eva to mull over the words.

How could she carry a child who might look like that man? Bea was right. Eva sank back down into the chair.

"How far gone are you, honey?"

"About two months."

"It's good you came to me when you did." Bea gave an approving nod. "This is the best time."

"What do you mean?"

"Less danger to you. Less mess."

Eva's stomach tightened at the callous words. What was it Aimee had said about God hating hands that shed innocent blood?

The teakettle whistled, and Eva jumped.

"Calm down, little one. You'll likely jump out of your skin."

The woman seemed nice enough, but remembering Sally's warning about Bea's meanness, she resolved to remain on her guard.

Sally glanced at Eva. "Are you sure you want to go through with this? There are worse things in the world than having a baby."

Bea shoved her aside. "Leave the girl alone. What are you still doing here, anyway?"

"Making sure she's taken proper care of. She's a nice girl. Too nice to be held prisoner in a place like this."

Eva started. "Prisoner? What do you mean?"

Bea gave a short laugh. "Sally is always exaggerating. She used to work for me and always complained about my rules. But you aren't that kind of young woman, are you? You came here for help, which I'm happy to give." She set a cup of tea in front of Eva. "Drink this, my dear. It'll help you relax."

Though not fully satisfied with the answer, Eva took the tea, grateful for something to settle her stomach. "Thank you."

"Now I need to ask a few questions before I can give you the help you need. Do you have any friends or family members who are likely to come looking for you?"

"No one will come if I get back home soon. How long will this take?"

Bea looked sideways at Sally, but Eva couldn't decipher the meaning behind the frown.

"The procedure will be fairly quick. But you'll need to rest afterward. I normally keep someone like you in bed for a couple of days at least."

"Oh no. Rex would call on all of his connections to find

me if I were gone that long."

Were her words slurring? Eva grabbed hold of the table as the room began to spin. "I—I don't feel so good. Sally? I'm scared." She clutched at the woman's hand. "God hates hands that shed innocent blood. I don't want God to hate me. I love Him."

"It's all right. You don't have to do this."

"Shut up, Sally." Bea's voice rose in pitch. "What connections do you mean? Who is Rex?"

"My cousin's husband." Eva took a deep breath and laid her cheek on the table in front of her. "Rex Donnelly."

"The attorney?"

"Mm-hmm. He fights for the innocent. God hates hands that shed innocent blood." Eva began to sob. Her mind was whirling and confused, but she knew she couldn't kill the life within her. "I have to go. I can't do this. I can't murder an innocent baby." Suddenly she pitched forward, and darkness claimed her.

❧

He'd seen her walk into that saloon last night. But she never came out. Anger burned in his chest. She'd come to Oregon City to taunt him.

Oh, she would pay for this.

❧

Eva woke slowly. Her head pounded, and she was disoriented, in a strange bed, in unfamiliar surroundings. She tried to sit up, but a stab of pain sent her back to her pillow.

"Don't try to get up too soon. You've been out for a while."

She opened her eyes to the voice. "Where am I?"

Soft gray eyes looked down on her with kindness. "My

name is Martha O'Neill. My husband is the Reverend O'Neill. We serve the Lord by taking in women like you who are trying to change their ways."

"How did I get here?"

"We found you on the street yesterday morning. At first my husband thought you were dead, but when we got close, we could tell you were just unconscious. Drugged, most likely. We loaded you into our wagon and brought you here."

"Yesterday morning?" Eva sat up quickly, then moaned as pain stabbed her once more. A flash of pink caught her eye, and she glanced down at her dress. "What on earth?" How had she come to be wearing Sally's dress? Not a dress, really; more like a costume. An extremely indecent one at that. She grabbed the blanket and pulled it up to her chin.

"Modesty is returning already. How wonderful. The reverend and I would like to offer you a place to call home if you are willing to end your life of sin and learn to walk in the light of God's love and goodness. If you would prefer to be returned, you may have a good, hearty breakfast first, and afterward, my husband will drive you back to where he found you."

The woman gave her a soft, loving smile and placed her hand on Eva's cheek. "I can see you've been through a lot, child. Perhaps God brought you to us for a reason. Will you give Him a chance to show you true love?"

Eva grabbed Mrs. O'Neill's hand and held it close. "Thank you," she whispered.

"The love of God brought you here. My husband and I are only His hands and His feet."

"Oh, Mrs. O'Neill, if only I could believe in God's love again."

"You will, child. God has led you beside still waters so that He can restore your soul. You may stay with us for however long it takes God to do His work of restoration."

thirteen

It was all Jonesy could do not to grab Billy by the front of his shirt and throw him into the wall to make him understand. "We have to go after her."

Billy's eyes flashed, and he slapped his hand down on the desk. "Do you think I don't want to go find my baby sister?"

"Not from the looks of it. It's been two weeks, and I'm tired of waiting."

"Rex has hired four private detectives, and he called in favors at the sheriff's office in Oregon City. Right now I have my hands full with those horse thieves. The circuit judge is going to be coming through any time. I can't leave my post."

Jonesy slammed his fist against the wall. The pain came as a welcome relief against the ache in his heart. His Eva, missing, and no one could find her. What if she was gone for good? What if she was dead? Only the fact that the road between here and Oregon City was washed out had kept him from riding there as soon as he received word that she was missing.

He was about to appeal to Billy again when the door flew open. "Sheriff!" The bespectacled postmaster rushed inside and thrust a letter into Billy's hands. "I would have waited to give it to your pa and ma, but I know how anxious you all are to hear from Eva."

Jonesy's heart leaped. "That's from Eva?"

"Yes."

Billy stared at the envelope. "It's postmarked Oregon City."

"So much for four detectives and the sheriff's office."

A shrug lifted Billy's shoulders. "I'll get this out to Ma and Pa right away. Thank you, Travis."

"You're welcome, Sheriff."

"What are you waiting for?" Jonesy asked. "Open it."

"It's addressed to my parents. I'm not opening it."

Jonesy fought to keep from ripping it out of his hands. "All right then, let's go."

Billy grinned. "Let's."

They raced over slippery, muddy roads the five miles to Andy and Hope Riley's home. Both men reined in their horses at the same time and dismounted in record time. The door opened before they could make it to the porch.

"What are you two up to, tearing into the yard like that?" Mrs. Riley demanded. "Look at the marks you've left. Now the ground is going to dry with holes in it."

"Sorry, Ma. But I think you'll forgive us when you see what we brought you." Billy waved the envelope. "Word from Eva."

Andy stood behind his wife. "Oh, praise You, Lord."

Hope took the letter in shaking hands and looked at Billy with pleading eyes. "What does she say?"

"I didn't read it, Ma. It wasn't sent to me."

"Come inside. We'll open it in there."

In two minutes, they were sitting around the table. Mrs. Riley carefully opened the envelope and pulled out a piece of crisp white paper.

Dear Ma and Pa,

I'm so sorry for worrying everyone. I can only imagine how frantic you've been. Especially you, Ma. I have so much to tell you, and I will, as soon as I return. But for now, I'm staying with an elderly minister and his wife. They help women who need help. I won't go into details about how I came to be with these wonderful people, but please believe me that God brought me here. I'm safe and well cared for.

I need this time. Whether I will stay until the baby's born or even longer, I don't know. But I will write often. Please do not try to find me. Be comforted in knowing that I'm in good hands.

Lovingly,
Your daughter, Eva

P.S. Tell Jonesy he was right. I was led beside still waters, and God is restoring my soul.

Tears misted Jonesy's eyes. "I guess God can take care of her better than I can. I just wish she would have told us where she is so we can at least see her."

"I think that's the point, Jonesy," Hope said softly. "Sometimes we just have to let go and hope our loved ones come back to us."

Andy nodded. "Eva's got a lot of my ways in her. She has to figure things out on her own just like I did."

"Like you, sir?" Jonesy's heart picked up at the look of love that passed between Eva's parents.

"I had my difficult days of trying to understand why certain things happen in life. I blamed God and grew bitter just like my daughter has. I had to go away and spend a winter in the mountains with a mountain man and his Indian wife to find God's purpose for me."

Hope took his hand. "He came back to me just before Eva was born."

"Do you think Eva will come back to me?"

"The most important thing right now is that she's setting her heart back to trusting God's love for her. Whether she'll ever trust yours is something to be determined later."

❧

Eva had been at the O'Neills' for less than a month when she was finally able to keep down a full meal. Her energy returned, and she found the routine quite to her liking. Along with doled-out chores, Reverend O'Neill gave a daily devotion in the chapel, tucked inside an arbor of evergreens.

Mrs. O'Neill ended each day's scripture reading by playing a hymn on her organ and allowing the Word to settle into their minds. On Sunday, the three families close enough to come to services during the winter made the trip and joined the O'Neills and their girls.

Eva, along with two other women, occupied a spare room in the cozy log cabin. It was a little cramped, but Eva didn't care. She loved the solitude of the cabin. Loved looking outside the door and seeing the snowcapped mountains in the distance.

She felt a little guilty for not admitting to them that she wasn't a prostitute in need of redemption. Some days she felt as though she were taking their kindness under false pretenses.

Millie and Shawna were there for the right reasons. Millie was an old prostitute who had been beaten and left for dead. Shawna had been kidnapped in England when she was fourteen years old and brought over on a ship of white slaves. She hadn't seen her parents in ten years and had no desire to return to England. But her soul was prospering under the kind tutelage of the O'Neills.

She had arrived much the same way Eva had, four months earlier. She'd already given her heart to one of the young men who attended services. Eva could see he shared her affection, but under his mother's watchful eye, the two never seemed to have the opportunity for more than a few cursory words.

Eva's other roommate, Millie, fought a little harder against the restrictions. She'd lived in a drunken fog for so long that facing the clarity of real life seemed difficult for her.

Eva lay in bed, looking at the stars through her window. She was glad she got the bed next to the window. Leaving the house was still a fearsome thing for her, but staring at the stars each night was almost like being outdoors. She longed for Patches and the midnight rides they used to take when the moon was bright and the terrain free from mud or ice. Poor Patches. How was he doing?

"*Psst.* Shawna, Eva."

Eva sat up. "What's wrong, Millie?"

"I'm leavin'."

"What do you mean?" Shawna's hint of an English accent, left over from childhood, always made Eva ache for Jonesy and his penchant for sliding into the accent. Only since meeting Shawna had Eva realized how brilliantly he'd accomplished it.

Millie lit the candle next to her bed. "Listen, ladies. If the three of us started our own business, we could split it three ways and take care of each other."

Leave it to Millie to think of an enterprise. Eva had trouble thinking beyond today. "You mean like sewing dresses? My aunt was a seamstress in her day. I'm sure she'd give us some advice."

Millie chortled. "You're a right funny one. A seamstress. You know good and well what I'm talking about."

"You two can do whatever you want," Shawna said with unaccustomed force, "but I'm never going back to selling myself. I'm living for God now, and I might even be getting married one day."

At the realization of what Millie wanted her to do, Eva's jaw dropped. A gasp escaped her throat, and heat rushed to her cheeks. After living with these women for a month, she thought she was past embarrassment at the mention of their former lifestyles, but judging from her shock, she was far from past anything.

"Millie, you mustn't think of going back to your old life."

"It's all I know. I been in this business in one form or another for thirty years."

"But surely you don't miss it," Shawna said softly. "The O'Neills are so kind. And have you ever in your life heard stories like the ones they read to us from the Bible?"

"They's good people," Millie agreed. "I ain't sayin' they ain't. And livin' here is fine. . .for now. But what about when they need the bed space for another lost soul? Are they gonna let you stay on? I don't think so. And when it's time, where are you gonna go? Is some farmer really gonna marry a woman that ain't untouched? Is Mark's ma really gonna let him marry you?"

"I don't know." Shawna's lip trembled. "But even if it's not him, I hope to marry and have children someday."

A loud snort filled the room as Millie started to laugh. "I've known a lot of men in my day, and let me tell you. Ain't one of 'em any different from the others. They don't want girls like us for marryin'. A man wants a young thing he can take straight from her parents' home to his bed."

"Millie, not all men are that way." Eva's heart pounded in her chest. "There is a man back home who wants to marry me, even though he knows I'm not. . .pure."

"Back home?" The older woman's sharp gaze stabbed into Eva's. "I thought you was from Oregon City."

Swallowing hard, Eva fought for a reply.

Fortunately, a tap on the door silenced the conversation. "Ladies?" Mrs. O'Neill came in. "You're up late. Is there a problem?"

"No, ma'am," Eva said. "Did we wake you?"

She let out a laugh. "I'm looking for the reverend's spectacles. He's laid them down again. That man. If he hadn't married me, he'd be half blind all the time."

The comment brought out laughter around the room. "We were just discussing marriage," Eva said. "You and Mr. O'Neill seem so happy."

A smile spread across the gentle face. "Marriage is the most wonderful relationship God ever created."

"God made marriage?" Shawna's eyes grew wide. "Does the Bible say that?"

"Of course. God saw that it wasn't good for man to be alone, so He took a rib from Adam's side and created a bride for him. It also says that the marriage bed is undefiled. And that a man shall leave his father and mother and cleave to his wife."

"That sounds wonderful." Shawna's eyes grew dreamy in

the soft glow of the candlelight. "What's the name of the man who wants to marry you, Eva?"

"Jonesy." A smile tipped Eva's lips at the thought of his handsome face.

"Tell us about him," Mrs. O'Neill encouraged, sitting on the edge of Eva's bed.

So she did. She told them about his silliness. His fake accents. Lord Byron the dog. Lady Anne the horse. His love for poetry. And how he'd asked her to marry him even though she wasn't pure.

The elderly woman patted her hand. "And why did you refuse him?"

Eva looked at her hands, twisting the blanket. "I'm not really ready to talk about that."

"There's no need to. That's between you and the Lord."

Mrs. O'Neill looked at all three. "I want you to remember the scripture we read this morning from Second Corinthians. 'If any man be in Christ, he is a new creature'—and that goes for women, as well. 'Old things are passed away; behold, all things are become new.' The world may see you as used up. Old before your time. But God wants to give you back the days the devil has stolen from you. You're not impure anymore. God can bring a man into each of your lives who will love you unconditionally, despite past mistakes."

Millie gave another loud snort, turned over on her bed, and pretended to be asleep in moments.

Mrs. O'Neill stood and walked toward the door. "Well, I suppose I'll go back to bed. You girls try to go to sleep now, all right?"

"Yes, ma'am."

In the morning, Millie was gone. And so was fifty

dollars that Mrs. O'Neill kept tucked away in a jar in the cabinet. Eva's locket was also missing. As much as she regretted that Millie had stolen the locket Pa had given her, she regretted even more that the woman had chosen to return to her old life.

"Jesus knew that His listeners wouldn't all accept His truth," the kindly reverend said with a sad shake of his head. "We'll continue to pray for Millie until the Lord releases us from the burden."

They bowed their heads and did just that.

Eva had never known such peace.

She had not yet told the O'Neills about her pregnancy. Deep inside, she feared they would turn her out if they knew. She couldn't help but smile at the irony. If she were a woman of ill repute, she could stay. But as merely a wounded soul, the victim of a brutal attack, this wasn't the place for her.

Christmas came and went, and February was now upon them. When Eva lay in bed at night, she could feel her bulging stomach. Soon her condition would be visible through her petticoats and thick skirts. She'd have no choice but to tell the O'Neills. She only hoped when the truth came out, they would allow her to stay and complete the healing God had begun in her.

One night, she was just finishing up a letter to home when a knock sounded on the door. Mrs. O'Neill entered upon Eva's welcome. "Hello, girls."

No matter that Eva was nineteen and Shawna five years older, to Mrs. O'Neill they were mere girls. "The reverend will be going to Oregon City tomorrow morning for supplies. If you'd like to mail a letter, or if you need anything in particular, let him know tonight."

"I have a letter to send." Eva took the addressed envelope from under her pillow. "I—I don't have the price of postage."

"It's all right. You've earned it in the chores you do around here. Always doing more than we ask of you."

"Thank you, ma'am. My ma raised her children to keep up with tasks." Eva took a deep breath. "Mrs. O'Neill, there is something else I'll be needing, but I don't know how to go about asking for it."

"What is it?"

Casting her glance to the quilt, Eva began to tremble.

"What's wrong, dear?"

"I—I need to begin sewing some things for. . .my baby. You see, I—I am with child."

"Oh, honey, I'm so sorry. Imagine you bearing this burden alone for all these weeks. Don't worry. You're not the first girl to come to us in this condition. We have baby clothes in the loft, along with a cradle and some blankets."

Relief washed over Eva. "Thank you, ma'am."

"We can still buy some material for you to make your baby a couple of new gowns, too. Would you like that?"

Eva shook her head. "There's no need to go to any trouble or expense. I'm sure the clothes you have are fine."

"Oh, Eva." Shawna's eyes glowed with the look of a woman who couldn't wait to be a mother. "Imagine having a baby to hold and love."

"I'm not exactly in a position to be a mother," she said bitterly.

"Don't you worry," Mrs. O'Neill broke in. "You're going to be a wonderful mother. I've seen it before. The woman isn't sure until that baby makes his entrance into the world.

Then all that matters is that sweet little face."

Eva looked into the woman's smiling eyes and knew she had to come completely clean. "My baby was conceived in rape, Mrs. O'Neill. I wasn't a prostitute. I was a proper girl from a good family. I went riding alone one night when I shouldn't have. I almost died, but Jonesy rescued me."

"A hero," Shawna said breathlessly.

"Oh, Shawna, please."

"But why were you dressed in such a manner when my husband discovered you?"

Tears flooded Eva's eyes. "I had gone to that section of town to find someone who could help me get rid of the baby."

Shawna gasped. "Eva, that's dangerous. I've seen many women almost die from that."

"What happened that you didn't go through with it?" Mrs. O'Neill gently prodded.

"The woman must have slipped something into my tea, because I started feeling strange. I remember telling them I couldn't take the baby's life and risk shedding innocent blood. They asked me about my family. That's the last thing I remember."

"Who is your family, Eva? Is there some reason those people would dump you in the street dressed like a saloon girl? They must have been scared. Otherwise they'd have just killed you."

"My cousin Aimee is married to Rex Donnelly, an attorney."

Shawna shifted on her bed. "He's a famous one, too. Be glad of it. From what I hear, Bea is a rough character. She forces girls to work for her and only lets them go if they're about ready to die or if someone offers the right price."

Eva thought of Sally from Mike's place. If only she could bring her to the O'Neills.

Eva's memory of the conversation between Bea and Sally made sense now. Sally had stayed that morning to make sure Bea didn't try to keep Eva there against her wishes.

"Eva, why did you try to take your baby's life?"

Eva looked at her through eyes blurred from tears. "I don't want to raise a baby who I might resent. Now I have no choice."

"There is always a choice, honey."

It took a moment for Mrs. O'Neill's words to make sense.

"Oh no. I couldn't take him to an orphanage. My aunt and uncle run one. They do their best to take care of all the children they take in. But it never seems as though they can do enough. A baby needs to be held much more than an orphanage can provide with such limited staff."

"What about finding a married couple who might take the baby in and raise him as their own?"

Eva jerked her head up to look at Mrs. O'Neill. "I hadn't thought about that. Do you think. . ." She drew a deep breath. "Do you think it's all right if I do that?"

"Giving your baby to a loving family rather than trying to love someone who reminds you of the agony you endured?" Mrs. O'Neill looked at Eva through eyes filled with compassion. "I think perhaps the Lord brought you here for more than one reason."

"What do you mean?"

"To help heal your pain from the ordeal you've been through, of course. But perhaps also for Lissa and Amos Matthews."

"Who?"

"They've been married for close to ten years, but God hasn't blessed them with any children of their own. They live a little far away, so they don't normally attend Sunday services until after the spring thaw."

A sense of relief filled Eva. It seemed God had provided a way for her to give birth to the baby and yet be free of the constant reminders she would have if she raised the child. In a few months, she could go home and resume her life.

fourteen

Dear Pa and Ma,

Every day brings us a little closer to all-out spring. It's hard to believe April has already arrived. The snow is melting, and yesterday I saw a bud on a rosebush. It won't be long now. You know how much I love roses.

I have come to a decision of which I've been trying to inform you for a few months now, but the words just never seemed sufficient. Perhaps they still aren't, but I feel I must go ahead, even at the risk that it will sound callous.

I've decided to give the baby to a childless couple. I believe God brought me here so I could give them the child growing inside me. I know I can't love it the way a child needs to be loved.

I hope you can forgive me for giving the baby away. I do feel that I am making the right decision, and I beg you to understand.

Eva

P.S. Tell Jonesy I saw a flock of geese returning today. I took some stale bread and gave them a welcome-home party.

Jonesy smiled at the memory of Eva telling him she used to send the geese off for the winter with full stomachs. Oh, how he missed their rides together, their talks.

Each time the Rileys received a letter from Eva, they sent

for him and allowed him to sit and listen while Hope read. A new letter had arrived at least once a month, and each carried a P.S. for him.

Despite his joy that she'd sent him another personal message, he felt heartsick that she would give away her child. If only she knew that he was willing to marry her and take her away. Be a pa to the baby. Frustration clamped tightly around his middle. How could he prove his love for her if she wouldn't tell anyone where to find her?

He'd missed the April first deadline he'd given himself to go back to Texas. Here it was, the middle of May. It always took a couple of weeks for one of Eva's letters to reach them in Hobbs. If she came back late in the summer, they would still have time to leave. Otherwise they would have to wait through one more winter. It would be too risky to leave in the fall, especially with a baby—and that was if he could find Eva before she went through with her plan to give the child away.

Jonesy had been so deep in his thoughts that he hadn't noticed Mrs. Riley lean against Mr. Riley's shoulder. Tears flowed down her cheeks.

"Mrs. Riley," Jonesy said with conviction, "I'm going to Oregon City. I have to find Eva and convince her not to give the baby away. I still want to marry her. I'll raise that child as my own."

Mr. Riley regarded Jonesy evenly. "But she's asked us not to try to find her. She seems to be doing well, and I want to give her time to sort all this out. I think you should, too."

Hope reached across the table and patted Jonesy's hand. "I believe Eva's made a wise choice in turning the baby over to parents who will love him fully."

"But I'd love the baby just as much. There's no need for Eva to do this."

The Rileys remained silent.

He said his good-byes in short order, then rode to his parents' house to relay the contents of the letter to his ma. "I need to find her," he said. "But Mr. Riley believes I have no business trying to."

"He's right," Ma said softly. "Give it some more time, son. She'll come home when she's ready."

"But it'll be too late by then. She'll have already given the baby away."

"Why are you so set on raising this child? Are you afraid that if Eva doesn't keep the baby, she won't need you to marry her and sweep her away to Texas?"

Jonesy cringed at his mother's words. "Of course not."

At least that's what his mind screamed. But as he went about doing his chores, somewhere deep down inside, he knew she was right.

Charity suffereth long and is kind. It seeketh not her own.

He wanted Eva to need him. So much so that he resented her desire to share the baby with a barren couple. "Oh, God. Forgive me."

Peace swept over Jonesy. But the urgency to find Eva seemed to intensify in that moment. He knew that as surely as the earth needs water, Eva needed him. He also knew that God was telling him to go find her.

❧

Pete sat at the bar next to Randy and slugged down another whisky. After being cooped up in this town all winter and spring, he was plenty restless. He made a grab for the nearest woman, a plump but pretty saloon girl.

She gave him a slow smile with luscious, stained lips. "What can I get for you, Cowboy?"

A flash of gold around her neck arrested his attention. He frowned. It looked familiar. He made a grab at it and snatched it in his fingers before she could stop him.

"Hey, mister, that's mine. And Mike don't take kindly to us gettin' manhandled. Ain't that right, Mike?"

"Leave her locket alone, mister."

"I want to know where she stole this from. I know the owner."

The prostitute sneered. "I didn't steal it. Eva gave this to me."

"It was a gift from her pa," he growled. "She wouldn't have given it away."

"Okay, fine. Keep it."

"I don't want the locket. I want the girl. Where is she?"

"Why should I tell you?"

"Let's just go," Randy said quietly. "You don't want to start that trouble again."

Pete moved slowly away. Randy was right, for now. He had ways of getting information out of women. This cow would tell him where to find Eva, or she'd be dead by morning.

fifteen

Lady Anne carried Jonesy into Oregon City just as dawn was beginning to break. He'd left directly after supper, under protest from his parents, and had ridden all night. Before he left, he'd stopped by the Rileys to let them know he was going. He'd felt it was the right thing to do. After all, Eva was their daughter and they had requested that he not go. But something in Andy's eyes shone his approval when they'd shaken hands. "I'd be doin' the same thing if it were my Hope."

Those words of assurance had been all the confirmation Jonesy needed that going to Oregon City was the right decision.

Mrs. Riley handed him an envelope. "Go to our niece Aimee's house. The address is on the back of that letter. Rex can tell you where to find Eva."

Jonesy stared at the envelope, trying to wrap his mind around the truth of Hope Riley's words. "You've known all along where she is?"

She nodded. "Rex's private investigators found her before Eva's first letter arrived."

"And you never brought her home?" Jonesy said, a bit too harshly.

Mr. Riley had placed a protective arm about her shoulders. "We knew she was safe. And she needed some time away."

"Then why are you telling me now?"

"If you're determined to find her, there's no sense in sending you on a wild-goose chase. What happens between the two of you is something you'll have to sort through. It's not our place to deliberately keep you from her."

Jonesy followed the directions on the back of the letter and by morning had found the place. A servant answered his knock.

"Is this the home of Rex and Aimee Donnelly?"

The stiff male servant nodded. "Who may I say is calling?"

"Ben Jones. I'm a friend of Aimee's aunt Hope and uncle Andy. I have a letter for Aimee from Eva's parents."

He took the envelope and stepped away from the doorway. "Come inside, please." He led the way to an elegantly furnished sitting room and waved Jonesy inside. "Wait here, please. I will inform Mr. and Mrs. Donnelly of your presence."

"Thank you."

In moments, they appeared. The man shook his hand, and the lovely woman with blond curls and blue eyes offered her hand, as well.

"Thank you both for seeing me."

"I read Aunt Hope's letter. Eva is very blessed to have a man who loves her so much."

"I'm the one who feels blessed to know her. I need to find her." He looked from one to the other. "Can you please lead me in the right direction?"

Rex sat next to Aimee on the settee. "She's living with a minister and his wife about four hours' ride north. There is a small community of farmers who gather to worship at Reverend O'Neill's chapel on Sunday. They seem to make a habit of taking in strays like Eva."

Jonesy's ire rose. "Eva's far from being a stray."

Rex gave a chuckle. "Believe me, I didn't mean to insult her. I just meant they seem to take in people who don't have anywhere else to go. If Eva was looking for solitude and kindness, that's why she ended up with the O'Neills and why she's stayed with them for so long."

Mollified, Jonesy let down his guard. "I'm grateful to them for helping her and keeping her in a safe place, but it's time to find her."

Jonesy received instructions on which road to take out of town and how to find the little log cabin and chapel in the woods.

Aimee insisted he join them for breakfast. Jonesy had to admit he felt better and more energized after the meal. His hopes were high as he set out to find Eva.

❧

The sun had already risen by the time Eva opened her eyes and greeted the day. Her back ached before she even moved. She would be so relieved when the next two months were over and her body returned to normal. To have energy again. To be able to sleep all night without visiting the outhouse. To do something as simple as shifting from side to side without effort.

Her bulging stomach rolled as the baby moved inside her. She smiled. "You're just waking up, too, huh, little one?"

Shawna entered the room, smiling brightly. "Oh, good. You're up. Mrs. O'Neill says you should get ready soon or you'll be late for morning services."

Stretching and yawning, Eva heaved up to a sitting position. "I feel as though I haven't slept a wink."

"I heard you get up at least three times." Sympathy sang

in her tone. "Don't worry. It'll all be over soon. The baby will be tucked away safe and sound at the Matthewses' home. Then you can forget this ugliness ever happened to you."

Forget? Though the memory had faded and the terror diminished each day as the peace of God reigned in her life, Eva knew she'd never forget the horror of that night. But over the past months, she had come to understand that God was able to carry her through. That every day didn't have to be about what had happened to her. She knew that once the baby was born, she would be ready to go home.

❧

Smoke curled into the air above the little log cabin. From the edge of the woods thirty yards away, Pete watched a small dog playing with a fallen branch. He scanned the surrounding area to see if there were any larger dogs that might be a problem.

The door opened, and a pretty young woman appeared. She smiled and stooped down to pet the dog. Pete glanced at Randy. "Looks like there's one for you, too."

"Shut up," Randy snarled. "I like my women willing. I don't force myself on them."

Pete bristled at the accusation. Randy didn't understand the special relationship he had with Eva Riley. He drew in a breath when the door opened again. His dark-haired beauty appeared. Pete frowned. She looked. . .different.

"Aw, she went and got fat. Why would she do that when she knows I'm coming back to her?"

His companion shook his head. "There ain't no helpin' you, Pete. You belong in an asylum somewhere."

"You tellin' me she don't look fat to you?"

"Idiot. The only thing big on that girl is her stomach, and there's only one reason for that."

Pete gave a snort. "Yeah, too much food."

Randy looked away in disgust. "If you don't like fat women, why not just let her go?"

"Let her go? She's been waitin' for me all this time. How would it look if I got this close and then just left without seein' her?"

"Are you crazy?" Randy growled, his voice as angry as Pete had ever heard. "You forced yourself on that girl. She's praying she never sees your ugly face again."

"Shut up!" Pete felt the blackness coming. He didn't like it and tried not to do what it wanted, but usually he couldn't help himself. Pictures played in his head, and he had to do what he saw. He raised his gun and slammed it down on the back of Randy's neck. The man slumped forward with an *oomph*, then slid from his horse.

Poor Randy. He didn't understand how Pete felt about Eva. He'd been a good friend, but Pete couldn't take a chance the burly man would disrupt his plans. Not when he was this close to getting what he wanted.

❧

Eva gathered a deep breath of rain-soaked air as she headed down the path to the chapel. She would be the last one to arrive, as was becoming a habit. Since Mrs. O'Neill had released her from morning chores during the past month, she'd allowed herself those few coveted extra moments of sleep.

The organ music was already playing before she was even halfway up the tree-lined path. Suddenly, above the music, she heard the reverend's voice.

"Fear thou not; for I am with thee: be not dismayed; for I am

thy God: I will strengthen thee; yea, I will help thee; yea, I will uphold thee with the right hand of my righteousness."

Eva frowned. How could it be that she heard the reverend's voice so clearly above the congregation singing "Blessed Assurance"?

She heard it again.

"Fear thou not; for I am with thee: be not dismayed; for I am thy God: I will strengthen thee; yea, I will help thee; yea, I will uphold thee with the right hand of my righteousness."

Footsteps behind her made her smile. The reverend must have forgotten his spectacles again. The scripture she heard him reciting was surely his text. Without his eyeglasses, he wouldn't have been able to read a word.

Her smile widened, and teasing bubbled to her lips. She turned to greet him.

Disbelief shot across her mind. Her forward momentum halted midstride, and she backed up. A scream tore at her throat, but no sound emerged.

Him! No! He couldn't have found her.

His eyes flashed with evil intention. "Hi, Eva. Did you miss me?"

He reached out and grabbed her wrist, pulling her to him. Pressing his mouth close to her ear, he whispered, "Don't make a sound."

Hot tears burned her eyes. She knew she wouldn't live this time.

❧

Jonesy heard the sound of singing and an organ playing in the distance. His heart skipped. In moments, he would see his beloved Eva again. All the way from town, he'd tried to imagine what he would say to her. Especially when he knew she didn't want to see him.

He wasn't even sure why he'd come at this point. He wouldn't try to talk her out of giving up her baby. He wouldn't ask her to come to Texas with him. He had decided he wouldn't ask her to marry him until he knew she was ready.

For now, he had every intention of keeping his word that they would go back to their easy friendship. The one they'd shared before admitting their feelings for each other.

Lady Anne stamped her legs and whinnied as they neared a clearing in the woods. "What is it, girl?"

Jonesy heard a man moaning. "Hello? Is someone there?"

"Help," came the feeble reply.

Jonesy halted Lady Anne and dismounted. He walked toward the moaning. "Where are you?"

"Here."

Drawing in a breath, Jonesy recognized the man on the ground. Blood stained his shirt and the back of his head. "Randy? What are you doing here?"

"Pete found her."

Fear exploded in his chest. "What?"

"Eva's in danger. Hurry."

"Where?"

"I ain't sure." Randy grimaced.

"If you've hurt her, I'll kill you!"

"I tried to talk him out of it. That's the only reason I came along. So I could try to protect her for you. But he must have figured it out, 'cause soon as my back was turned, he knocked me in the head." He moaned again. "We saw her come out of the house."

Alarm burst through Jonesy. "Did he figure out that she's. . . ?"

"That dimwit thought she was fat. I tried to tell him, but he couldn't figure it out."

Jonesy blew a relieved breath. He looped Lady Anne's reins around a nearby tree and drew his pistol. "Look out for my horse," he told Randy. "I'll be back to help you as soon as Eva's safe."

Slowly he moved toward the clearing. Several yards of land lay between him and the house where he would be visible to anyone watching. "Lord, please keep me hidden," he whispered.

He traveled swiftly across the open land to the cabin. With his back against the log wall, he made his way around to each window. He could see no one in the cabin.

He forsook the path and used the trees as shields as he headed toward the chapel.

"Fear thou not; for I am with thee. . . ." The sound of Eva's voice reached his ears. "Be not dismayed; for I am thy God."

"Shut up!" Pete's voice sounded wild with anger. "I said, shut up!"

When Jonesy spotted him, his heart nearly stopped. Eva sat beside him, bound to a tree. What could Pete possibly be thinking? If he wanted to kidnap her, he could have been long gone by now. If he wanted to hurt her again, or even kill her, he could have done that, too. But to tie her up not far from the chapel, where people were bound to hear her if she screamed? It made no sense.

"I will strengthen thee; yea, I will help thee."

"Stop it! I can't think." Pete covered his ears and squeezed his eyes shut.

Eva's voice trembled, and Jonesy could see she was fighting to believe her own words. "I will uphold thee with the right hand of my righteousness."

"Stop it!" Pete pointed the gun toward Eva's head. "I mean it. I'll kill you."

"No!" Jonesy rushed forward as Pete swung around. A shot rang out.

Pete dropped. Jonesy looked down at his still-cold pistol. He hadn't even been able to think clearly enough to fire. How. . . ?

"Jonesy!" Eva's scream pierced the air. "Behind you!"

He turned just in time to see Randy, gun in hand, crumple to the ground at his feet. His eyes closed, but his chest rose and fell in shallow breaths.

"It's all right, Eva. He saved us." Jonesy quickly closed the distance between them and began working the knots in the ropes that bound her wrists behind the tree. "Pete knocked him out earlier, when he was going to try to save you. He's lost a lot of blood. Only God could have given him the strength to come find us, and just when we needed him."

"How did you find me?" she asked.

"Rex knew where you were."

Once she was free, he held back, unsure if she had digressed to the fear she'd experienced after the first attack.

But she smiled, her eyes shining with what he hoped was love, and threw her arms about his neck. "Oh, Jonesy, God told me He was sending help. He told me not to be afraid. And you came at just the right time."

Jonesy closed his eyes and held her, his heart swelling with love and relief that she was all right, in her soul and in her spirit.

She pulled away slightly and nodded toward Randy's still form. "Is he. . . ?"

"Just unconscious. But I'm not sure about Pete."

Jonesy stood and offered Eva his hand. She lumbered to her feet. His gaze slid across her middle. Her face grew red with shame. There were so many things he wanted to say to her. But for now, he had to attend to the two outlaws lying on the ground.

He slipped his arm about her shoulders. "Let's walk to the chapel where I can get a couple of men to help with those two."

Eva lay her head against his shoulder as they walked. For Jonesy, that small action on her part proved that she trusted him. And for this moment, that was all he needed.

sixteen

Eva wiped her damp palms on her dress and paced the room as the hour hand on Mrs. O'Neill's mantel clock turned past midnight.

"Don't worry, Eva," Mrs. O'Neill said softly. "They'll be back soon."

Eva sank into a chair next to the fireplace, but her gaze stayed fixed on the door.

"Your Jonesy loves you a great deal."

"Do you think he still does? Even after seeing me like this?"

Eva's heart nearly burst with love for Jonesy. Love she'd been unable to feel or release for so long. But seeing him again, feeling his arms around her, had made her see everything clearly.

"A person would have to be blind and deaf not to see the love in his eyes and hear the love in his voice."

The instant she heard the rattle of wagon wheels, she flew to the door and flung it open.

Jonesy jumped from the wagon before it stopped and snatched her up in an embrace. They stood motionless in each other's arms. He buried his face in her neck.

Only when Reverend O'Neill politely cleared his throat did Jonesy pull away. They entered the cabin and sat around the table. Mrs. O'Neill poured tea.

"What happened with Randy and Pete?" Eva asked.

"The doctor was able to pull them both through. Billy's been notified, but they'll stay in Oregon City to stand trial. They've done enough thieving in these parts to hang."

"Both of them?"

"I'm going to put in a good word for Randy. But I don't know how much good it's going to do."

"Thank the Lord everyone is all right," Mrs. O'Neill said, smiling.

Reverend O'Neill drained his cup and stood. "Well, I suppose I'll go bed the horses for the night."

His wife stood with him. "I'll help you."

"Help me?"

Her eyes widened, and she jerked her head toward Eva and Jonesy. Eva's cheeks warmed.

"Oh!" the reverend said. "Yes, good thinking. Come help me."

Eva dropped her gaze as the door closed behind them. She stood and began clearing the table. Jonesy's silence compelled her to venture a glance. Her heart sank as his eyes roved over her stomach.

"I didn't want you to see me like this. I was afraid of that look in your eyes."

He stood and closed the distance between them. "Sweetheart," he said, cupping her chin, "the only look in my eyes for you is love and admiration."

"Admiration?" She shook her head. "I'm carrying another man's child. How could you have anything for me but loathing?"

His thumb worked the soft skin along her jaw. "It doesn't matter how. All I know is that I love you more today than I ever have. And if you'll have me, I'll wait forever."

Her eyes misted with unshed tears, and her hand covered his. "Oh, Jonesy. You won't have to wait."

"Are you sure?"

She nodded. "I know I want to be your wife. I've known for quite some time."

"I want to take you and the baby with me to Texas."

Eva felt the blood drain from her face. "But. . .there's a couple here. . .Mr. and Mrs. Matthews. You met them at church today. I—I assumed Ma and Pa had told you I—"

"It's all right, Eva. This has to be your decision. And whatever you decide is all right by me."

"I believe God led me to the O'Neills for more than one reason. For one, I had to clear my head, away from my family. And even from you." Eva gathered in a deep, cleansing breath. "For another, so I could heal. And lastly, because the Matthewses are precious people who long for a child. I have such peace knowing the baby will be loved. And I love the baby enough to know that the Matthewses are the parents God has chosen to raise him."

Jonesy gazed at her with such tenderness that Eva nearly burst into tears of relief. She gave him a tentative smile. "Thank you for coming after me."

"I'll always be there for you. As long as you'll let me."

Eva raised her chin. "Kiss me, Jonesy."

Gently, almost cautiously, Jonesy dipped his head and briefly pressed his lips against hers.

"See?" she said. "No fear."

The corners of his mouth curved upward. "I love you."

Eva smiled and laid her head against his chest. "I love you, too."

❧

On Eva's wedding day, she carried the first roses of spring from her ma's rosebushes. The lace of her white gown trailed the ground as she walked along the path to the river's edge, clutching her pa's arm. Standing next to Gregory, Jonesy waited for her as the water rippled behind him. Handsome and tall, he wore the proudest look on his face that she'd ever seen.

She smiled as her pa lifted her veil and kissed her on the cheek before joining Ma, who stood with family members and close friends who had been invited to share in Eva and Jonesy's joyous day.

Eva's heart leaped at the look of utter delight on her groom's face as he took her hand and stepped forward.

They recited their vows with solemn reverence, and Eva knew as she listened to Jonesy's voice, husky with emotion, promising to love, honor, and cherish her all the days of their lives, that she had no need to ever fear him.

When she promised to love, honor, and obey her husband, and keep herself only for him, she meant it. Every word of it.

When at last they were pronounced husband and wife, Jonesy took her in his arms. His lips descended upon hers with tenderness, and Eva eagerly accepted his kiss. No fear quaked in her belly as it once had at the thought of closeness. Only peace for the life that lay ahead of them in Texas.

A Letter To Our Readers

Dear Reader:
In order that we might better contribute to your reading enjoyment, we would appreciate your taking a few minutes to respond to the following questions. We welcome your comments and read each form and letter we receive. When completed, please return to the following:

Fiction Editor
Heartsong Presents
PO Box 719
Uhrichsville, Ohio 44683

1. Did you enjoy reading *Beside Still Waters* by Tracey V. Bateman?
   ❑ Very much! I would like to see more books by this author!
   ❑ Moderately. I would have enjoyed it more if
   ____
   ____
   ____

2. Are you a member of **Heartsong Presents**? ❑ Yes ❑ No
   If no, where did you purchase this book? ______________
   ____

3. How would you rate, on a scale from 1 (poor) to 5 (superior), the cover design? ______________

4. On a scale from 1 (poor) to 10 (superior), please rate the following elements.

   ____ Heroine ____ Plot
   ____ Hero ____ Inspirational theme
   ____ Setting ____ Secondary characters

5. These characters were special because? ______________

____

____

6. How has this book inspired your life? ______________

____

____

7. What settings would you like to see covered in future **Heartsong Presents** books? ______________

____

____

8. What are some inspirational themes you would like to see treated in future books? ______________

____

____

9. Would you be interested in reading other **Heartsong Presents** titles? ❑ Yes ❑ No

10. Please check your age range:

❑ Under 18	❑ 18-24
❑ 25-34	❑ 35-45
❑ 46-55	❑ Over 55

Name ______________________________

Occupation ______________________________

Address ______________________________

City, State, Zip ______________________________

KANSAS HOME

4 stories in 1

Meet four survivors who've tossed social convention to the prairie winds in order to make their way on the frontier. Can these determined women open their lives to new possibilities in faith and love?.

Kansas Home is by accredited author Tracey V. Bateman.

Historical, paperback, 480 pages, 5 3/16" x 8"

Please send me ____ copies of *Kansas Home.* I am enclosing $6.97 for each. (Please add $2.00 to cover postage and handling per order. OH add 7% tax.)

Send check or money order, no cash or C.O.D.s, please.

Name____

Address______________________________________

City, State, Zip _______________________________

To place a credit card order, call 1-740-922-7280.

Send to: Heartsong Presents Readers' Service, PO Box 721, Uhrichsville, OH 44683